A Small Explosion

Also by Philip Purser

Peregrination 22
4 Days to the Fireworks
The Twentymen
Night of Glass
The Holy Father's Navy
The Last Great Tram Race
Where is He Now?
The One and Only Phyllis Dixey (*with* Jenny Wilkes)

A Small Explosion

by Graham L. Godley

Edited and Introduced by
Philip Purser

Secker & Warburg · London

First published in England 1979 by
Martin Secker & Warburg Limited
54 Poland Street, London W1V 3DF

Copyright © 1979 Philip Purser

SBN: 436 38825 1

Phototypeset in V.I.P. Palatino by
Western Printing Services Ltd, Bristol
Printed in Great Britain by
Redwood Burn Limited
Trowbridge and Esher

Introduction

I first met Graham Godley when he had contrived to upset a bowl of mayonnaise or something over his head. The spectacle of the gooey stuff slithering down his high forehead, into his trim little moustache and thence on to the white shirt and sober business suit that he was inappropriately wearing – considering the occasion was meant to be a 'swinging' party in the decade which took the same hideous adjective for its alliterative tag – was strangely unsettling. But for the grace of God and an extra two or three years of discretion might it not have been me simpering foolishly there, just as out of place among the loud voices and flowered shirts and see-through blouses all around? Luckily our hostess, who is presently identified as 'Binnie Davies', whisked him away before people in the other room could come whooping in, so that at least his wife didn't see his indignity, and when he reappeared a quarter of an hour or so later he seemed quite unabashed. Any lingering fellow-feelings on my part were obliterated when, smelling strongly of garlic (I see from his own account of the occasion, which incidentally confirms that he wasn't at all abashed, that it was an avocado dip and not merely mayonnaise with which he had anointed himself), he pinned me into a corner to talk about St Andrews University, where I had briefly played the part of an ex-service student. He had been there himself a little later. So had this Binnie person. We must all get together. Since I spent much of my time avoiding St Andreans and absolutely fleeing those who still clung to their student days as the high time of their lives, I wasn't very responsive. Besides, Godley was so stuffy and outer-suburban once he had recovered himself. He even tried to get me to go to church! How was I to know that in his car outside in the Beechway he was harbouring the device that was to set me this little literary task half a dozen years later?

I bumped into him again when he was trying to promote the children's book whose metaphor I have changed, in order to protect the innocent, into *Stanley the Suburban Squirrel*. He wanted me first to organize a feature on the *Telegraph* magazine, which I was able truthfully to say was impossible because he hadn't thought of it soon enough, and secondly to watch some television programme on which the book was being discussed. This I forgot to do. He had changed: the prim little moustache had gone: he was not so stuffy. He even said something quite funny about today's little innocent faces being tomorrow's clientele, though I see now that he had pinched it from Tom Lehrer.

It wasn't until we were about to leave the commuter village called 'Prickwell' in these pages, that I saw him for the last time. That would have been two years on again, the Spring of 1972. The 'For Sale' signs outside the house clearly disconcerted him. 'You're leaving too, then?' – 'Why? who else is?' He shrugged. 'Oh, everyone.' He had changed again. He was thin, nervous, rather naked. He wanted to know where I got my manuscripts typed. I told him about my Mrs Clark who lived over Henley way. Would she be able to transcribe a work which existed only on tape – specifically on the miniature cassettes of a pocket recorder? It was a sort of diary he had once kept. When I expressed some surprise that he wanted to go to the expense of transcription and typing for a private diary he said, 'Well, I suppose you might call it a work of fiction. Anyway, I want to have it done and read it, and then I'll see what to do with it, if anything.'

Somewhat against my better judgment I put him in touch with Mrs Clark, who could keep herself fully occupied with theses and dissertations she undertook through a contact at Oxford but always said she preferred typing a real book. Because I had been her very first author she always gave me priority and looked kindly on anyone I sent her way.

To take Godley on she had to equip herself with a transcription unit which would take his miniature cassettes, an expenditure which gave me a slight qualm straightaway. Moreover, when I called on her to say goodbye she let it be known that the cassettes Godley had delivered, the early ones, in particular, were hesitant and confused, with lots of ums and ers and instructions – usually too late to be helpful – to scrub the foregoing and start all over again. Once or twice the voice was slurred. Towards the end came some spools which were evidently the fruits of simply leaving the machine switched on to catch what it could, which in one case amounted to forty minutes of silence broken only by intermittent snores and peculiar grunts. Mrs Clark also intimated, in a voice I knew from the few occasions on which I had dared to give her something slightly raffish to type, that she couldn't say she was enjoying the substance of the narrative.

I had a renewed feeling that I had done her no great favour in giving her name to Godley. But it was to be three years before I saw her again and heard the end of the story, because characteristically she did not deign to mention the matter in the exchange of Christmas cards which, I regret to say, was our only intervening communication. As soon as she had finished the typing out Mrs Clark tried to telephone Godley. At first she got his wife, whom she described as sounding guarded; then it always seemed to be a child who answered the phone. Assurances that 'Daddy' would be given the message were never followed up by a call in return. Finally the number ceased to ring; a letter to Godley came back marked 'Gone away'.

Mrs Clark had invited me to read the transcript. I became quite intrigued by the story that unfolded. It occurred to me that with a little cleaning up and editing one would have – oh, dear: the third person impersonal is catching – we would have the up-to-the-minute equivalent of the novel that used to be couched in diary form, such as (at one extreme) the Swedish classic *Dr Glas* or (at the other), *Diary of a Nobody*. Indeed, this narrative may be said to fall somewhere between (if much below) the styles of Hjalmar Soderberg and the Grossmiths. If a publisher could be attracted, Mrs Clark might recoup some of her outlay on work and equipment.

The result also preserves, I thought, an accurate record of a particular society (commuter-belt bourgeois) at a time which, though only a few years past, already takes on a sort of faraway innocence. I have only concealed identities where this seemed advisable, and tidied up some repetitions and irrelevancies.

PHILIP PURSER

Chapter One

Testing one-two-three-four. My name is Graham Godley, aged forty years, blessed with a happy marriage and three adorable children – no, that won't do. Not that it is not true, of course; simply that it is something one might just as well write down or type or dictate to one's secretary. The whole point of this little gadget is that one must be spontaneous, one must commit one's immediate thoughts to it.

Exit Four ahead, London Airport. Then comes Three, Maintenance Area and Feltham and Staines, then Heston Services, then it's no distance really to the Chiswick Flyover . . .

But why say that today? Why say that any day? It's already in the A.A. Book.

Try again.

Imagine my surprise when Walter handed me a little package and said, 'Oh, I thought this might amuse you Graham . . .' But *who* am I telling this? Sorry, *whom?*

Walter brought you back from Hong Kong, so first of all perhaps I should introduce myself. My name is Graham Godley, aged forty . . .

5

Really, this is a total waste of time. One cannot confide in a machine. One needs a person in mind.

February 11

Memo: put car in for service as soon as possible, this week if Dino can oblige. There is definitely something amiss with the idling control.

February 13

One would have remembered anyway.

February 13 (p.m.)

Binnie Lines of all people! Wait till I tell Kate. On second thoughts, perhaps she wouldn't be very interested.

February 20

It was you! For a moment I thought it was Kate and was mystified as to how she could possibly have overtaken me. In any case, where would she be going at that time of morning? Then I remembered you also had a baby Fiat. Of course, there are enough of them about, once you start to notice them at all. There was no special reason to suppose it might be yours. Yet I had a funny feeling . . . could be coming from The Beechway, heading for the station . . . thought I'd hang back and see if it did turn into the station car park.

It must be the identical model to Kate's, Caravaggio blue with sun-roof. Hope I didn't cause any alarm, whooshing up behind you. It was just a spur-of-the-moment decision, in case you fancied a lift to town by car. You will have saved a few pence on the fare, even if a single back were ridicu-

6

lously expensive, because the 9.07 is too early for an off-peak return. One soon gets to know these little wrinkles.

But why should one search for excuses? It was well met, and great fun to have your company along the wretched motorway, or Autostrada del Slough as my neighbour Max Kennerly calls it! This is a play on 'Autostrada del Sole', which is in Italy. It means the 'Motorway of the Sun'.

I'm only sorry that your hair appointment was going to last right through the lunch hour. What on earth can they do that takes three hours, I always say to Kate. Never mind. Another time. At least we've established that Thursday is your usual day for London. It was last Thursday I put the car in for service and took the train, and in you popped just as it was moving, out of breath and with your ticket between your teeth but looking so alive, so colourful. I bet every man in the coach was staring. After nearly twenty years I knew who it was straightaway. Then you recognized me. What excitement! I think everyone must have been listening by then, as well as looking.

Binnie Lines. Don't I remember some story that you were named after Binnie Barnes? Or was it Binnie Hale? You had a stage-struck father or something like that.

Anyway, you finally got me going on this little gadget this morning when, looking for the ashtray, you opened the glove compartment and found it. 'What is it?' you demanded, without any of the diffidence most people would feel poking around in someone else's car. As I tried to explain, it's a little tape-recorder or 'electronic notebook' as they call them. My partner Walter Hale brought it back from Hong Kong on his last trip. They cost next to nothing there, it seems, despite being indistinguishable from the genuine article made by our worthy Dutch friends. One is supposed to carry it in one's vest pocket – if you remember, I made the point about the expression 'vest pocket' having always puzzled me as a boy because vests didn't have

7

pockets. Of course, it was an Americanism all the time, a 'vest' being a waistcoat there, but everyone happily referred to 'vest-pocket' diaries and flashlights and cameras and films without realizing this. I added that nowadays the younger generation probably don't know what our sort of vest is, since they never wear one and you said rather pointedly that you didn't either! Gosh, I suppose I did sound rather middle-aged. In point of fact I wear a Norwegian string vest, winter and summer, mainly for reasons of freshness. As for Kate's vests that I mentioned, well we both laughed but I would feel very disloyal if I let you go on thinking they are anything like those thick woolly garments you remembered from boarding school days and described so vividly! Hers are perfectly lacy and feminine. Indeed I sometimes wonder if they can make much difference to her being warm or not.

Anyway, whatever a vest is or was, a vest-pocket recorder makes quite a bulge in any decently cut suit. The idea of carrying it around at all times ready to press the button and dictate a memo to oneself is not really a very practical one. And although I've tried, I simply never remember to pack it in my document case; if I do, there never seems time to hunt for it. I'm afraid I'm not one of those systematic souls who go through life with a special wallet for their season ticket and a note of their blood group in case of accident! I heard of one chap from our neck of the woods who always carries a loaded camera in his car, so that if he's involved in a contretemps he can photograph the relative position of the vehicles, etcetera. Such foresight! But it gave me the idea of keeping the so-called electronic notebook in the glove compartment of the Three-Litre. If I had an accident, which Heaven forbid, it might be useful for obtaining eye-witness accounts and so forth.

More to the point, I've often noticed that when I'm driving home along the motorway my thoughts fall into place with a clarity which, alas, they've lacked during the day and seem to lose again as soon as I garage the car. Some little problem will suddenly appear quite simple, then next day it's as much of a muddle as ever. This wretched Mugwump business, for instance: tonight I see quite clearly that we have only to stand firm and rely on the moral correctness of the attitude I adopted, whatever Walter may say. One cannot go crawling to the Zillah Graves of this world, or where will it end?

Or sometimes an amusing version of one of the day's happenings will occur to me. I try it out to myself and the result is priceless. But when I pass it on to Kate and the children at the supper table, or perhaps reserve it for one of our little dinner parties, to which you and Geoffrey – you did say Geoffrey, didn't you? – will be invited in due course, more often than not the effect is disappointing. Again, one sometimes rehearses one's account of the day's doings in order to minimize certain aspects one would prefer not to be seized upon. Let me make it clear that Kate and I have been happily married for, oh fourteen years now and of course we have no real secrets from each other. But it can happen that in the interests of business one is obliged to entertain a buyer in what might sound rather a lavish style to the housewife mincing the remains of the Sunday joint to make a shepherd's pie!

Then there are artists to deal with and, now we're thinking of branching out rather excitingly, writers as well; and only the other day such a pretty little thing who came along to interview us for *Toys & Games*. Luckily, Walter does most of the foreign travel but there are toy fairs and exhibitions one had to attend; one cannot be too standoffish if the other chaps want to have a bit of a 'night out'.

And Kate is . . . well, at times she does have a caustic tongue. To tell the truth, it's that which has so far stopped me from telling her about meeting you. Ridiculous of me, I

9

know. I mean, it's a pure coincidence your coming to live in Prickwell – a happy coincidence, I hasten to add. And we happened to catch the same train that morning only because my car was in for a service and Kate needed the Fiat. Fancy you having the same little vehicle! They're great fun, I must say. We tease Kate about hers sometimes, the children and I – you know, have you wound it up, Mummy? That sort of thing. But they're just the things for buzzing round to coffee mornings and picking up from school and so on.

I *will* tell her, of course. For one thing, I shall want to be getting in touch with you both formally, to come round for a drink or a bite or one of our barbecue parties when summer comes. In the meantime please do ring me at the office next time you're in town, as you said you might, and we'll have a spot of lunch.

The trouble is that she (Kate) has heard your name when we've been in the company of St Andreans – she wasn't there herself: I sometimes wish she had been, she must feel a bit out of it at times. Fortunately, I'm not one of those people whose student days were the best of their life, etcetera, and are forever harking back to them. But Phil Purser, the local scribe was there, I'm told. Bill and Frieda Bellman are over at Twyford and Jess Judah, if you remember her, lives in Marlow and inevitably we get together occasionally. Wait till they hear you've come to swell the happy band.

Certainly you cut a dash at St A! And Kate knows we had a bit of a thing briefly, though I assure her it was quite innocent. As it was, worse luck! You got involved instead with that Lionel Brechin. There's also that mmm-mmm photograph of you as Charities Queen which I've kept in the album.

'Who's that?' the children always whoop, especially Miranda, who's the middle one and a little devil, she only does it to prompt the teasing of me she knows will follow. Children are like that, of course, as I'm sure you will know – I do look forward to meeting yours. I don't think you told me their names.

Anyway, Kate can be relied upon to say something mocking such as, 'Oh, that's daddy's glamorous girl friend when he was a student,' or 'That's the famous Binnie Lines.'

One time Little Sam, he's the youngest, made a quite startling remark about – well, about your figure. Heaven knows what they teach them in the schools these days. The *infant* school at that! It *was* rather amusing but Kate shouldn't have laughed. It only encourages precociousness. Of course, there may be more than a hint of the green-eyed monster there, she being slender herself.

I must say you've kept your figure, absolutely, as far as one could tell in outdoor clothes. One tends to assume that, um, well-developed girls will get a little thick after having babies and so on. I don't know why.

Motorway exit coming up. If I were to go through the industrial estate and along Boundary Road instead of round by the Priory, which is my usual route, I'd pass the top of The Beechway. Of course, I don't know the number, and you won't be in the book yet. Actually I've just realized that I don't even know your married name!

February 21

Played back the foregoing this morning and thought it encouragingly fluent, though I noticed I went off into a tangent as soon as I came to our meeting and never made the point I had intended to make, namely the object of the exercise!

As I was saying, I often feel that in these end-of-the-day meditations of mine I see things more clearly and put things more effectively than I do in company. When you lit on the

11

little recorder it suddenly occurred to me that if one formed the habit of recording something on the homeward journey every evening and then played it back next morning, it might be a useful exercise as far as improving the quality of one's self-expression and the clarity of one's thinking went. It is no trouble to reach into the cubby-hole. The only thing is that one must have some particular audience in mind. One cannot confide to an impersonal gadget.

It must be someone who is easy to talk to, who is not *too* close to one, i.e. dear Kate, and whose company one finds stimulating. You fit the bill on all three counts. I hope you don't mind! But of course you need never know.

It has only just struck me, incidentally, that it was needless of me to go on so about the nature of the little machine, as I did last night. If anyone were ever to listen to these thoughts, it would be self-evident as to how they had been recorded. As no one ever shall, it doesn't matter, does it?

February 25

I seem to have argued myself into a blind alley last time. To tell the truth, this ridiculous crisis with the Mugwumps has been coming to a head and I haven't been in the mood for soliloquizing for several nights now, though I suppose it is just the sort of problem I should try and talk over on the machine.

Did I tell you about the Mugwumps? I'm not one to bore others with details of one's business but you do know that my partner Walter Hale and I are in toys and games and so on. On leaving university, if you remember, I went off as a management trainee in Affiliated Newspapers, as was. Ended up in the promotions and exhibitions department. Oh, those concrete wastes of Earls Court and Olympia! And one could rely on the sturdy British workers downing tools on the eve of opening day so that there was no choice but to give in and pay them an extra bonus. Never mind, the Radio Show one year – it must have been one of the last times they held it, it's gone now – led to an invitation to join Avon Television on the merchandizing side. One had never realized what a profitable sideline it could be: the dolls and books and records they'd spin off from series like *Zap Squad* or *Space Hostess Trixie*, and all advertised for nothing!

It was Walter's idea that we should set up on our own. I had my doubts, I don't mind admitting, but it was a lucky move in that Avon lost their contract a couple of years later. We'd already managed to take quite a few of their agencies with us – I should explain that in our business we don't actually make anything, physically. We're agents, entrepreneurs or, as I prefer to regard it, ideas men. Actually it is a very creative activity. For example there is *Hawks and Doves*, the board game in which the players are superpowers armed with inter-continental missiles and nuclear submarines and spy planes and so on, which was all our own. It caught on especially well in the United States and we still draw a useful royalty from Parker there, not to mention one from Waddingtons over here. Then there's *Sabra*, a war-game which we based on the Six Days War and rushed into production within six months, believe it or not. Back in the toy field proper I am mulling over a little idea of my own which I'd rather play close to the chest for the moment, however silly it may seem to be secretive when no one is ever going to hear this!

But we are still very dependent on the merchandizing franchises, particularly all those stemming from the Mugwumps. I'm sure your children watch the show on television and have probably got all manner of the characters; stuffed, cut-out or injection-moulded, they all contribute their mite! Likewise the Mugwump books, Mugwump Weeny-Pops records, Mugwump nursery furniture, slide-projectors, tee-shirts and patches.

13

If ever they dropped the Mugwumps from TV we'd have to trim our sails pretty severely. Luckily there's always a fresh audience for them growing up, and any dwindling enthusiasm on the part of the BBC can usually be countered with a hint that the opposition is ready to snap up the prize. The trouble this time is that the annual bluffing match happens to coincide with some very tiresome behaviour from Zillah Graves, who thought them up in the first place. The Mugwumps, that is. She's got this wretched new husband – her third at the very least – who's been filling her head with over-inflated ideas as to their worth. Really, the ingratitude of some people would astonish you. Without us, she would still be churning out romantic fiction for the women's magazines. I told her as much and they both got very high-handed. Walter was away in Hong Kong at the time. Now he's implying that I didn't handle matters very diplomatically.

I'm sure they will climb down. But until they do it is impossible to play one side off against the other in our customary fashion. It *is* worrying. It would be idle to pretend otherwise.

The interesting thing is that it does look a little brighter simply to confess my worries. Of course, Kate will always listen and give advice, but she does get impatient very easily. I sometimes think she sees things *too* clearly!

I suppose this is the way out of that blind alley I ended up in last time. Even though you'll never hear these meanderings I have to pretend you will. Otherwise the exercise has no attraction.

February 26

Rather depressed tonight. The Mugwump business begins to weigh heavily. Zillah Graves and her wretched husband have been away in a cottage she has in the wilds of Wales for nearly a fortnight now, not even on the phone. I'm sure they did it deliberately. It is quite impossible to ring her up casually on some minor matter, such as the Finnish licence or similar, and test the atmosphere. As Walter says, a telegram would seem much too anxious.

Tomorrow is Thursday again. I wonder if you'll ring me about lunch.

February 27

You did! I really can't say if I expected it or not. I had a sort of nervous feeling half the morning. Every time the phone rang in the outer office I waited to see if Mrs Cernik would put it through to me or to Walter or deal with it herself. Once I thought I had perhaps missed the buzz and lifted my handset, and of course it was Mrs Cernik's daughter and they were having one of their long whispered conferences. I don't know what it was all about and certainly don't care – usually it's something to do with the daughter's unfortunate husband and what he has or hasn't been up to. Mrs Cernik invariably gets very hoity-toity if she thinks one is listening. I said as icily as I could, 'I'm sorry. I'm expecting a rather important call.'

Little did I know how right I was! Actually, I did mention it, though perhaps in a rather throwaway fashion. I didn't want to give the impression that only that was making me cheerful! Just before your call came Zillah Graves's, climbing down in a big way and more than ready to discuss reasonable terms. She asked for Walter, but he popped his head round the door to tell me.

'Vot a relief,' crowed Mrs Cernik, though I can't see it was any of her business. 'Mr Godley has been like a cat on 'ot tiles all the morning.'

'It certainly calls for a little celebration,' said Walter. 'What are you doing about lunch today, Graham?'

At which moment, precisely, you rang, which I hope will explain why I may have sounded a trifle confused at first. Especially as you merely said 'It's me'! Assuming I would know your dulcet tones straightaway! Actually on the phone your voice is not unlike Kate's, very nice and clear and sort of girlish.

Anyway, what a narrow squeak: thirty seconds later and I would have been committed to lunch with Walter at this Hungarian place he likes.

I see what you mean about Casa Nostra. There was a great deal of garlic in that bean dish, and at those prices one might have expected fewer beans and more good meat! Actually it's not a place I frequent, but I'd read about in the *Evening Standard*. Also it was handy for Goodge Street where I had to take Janet's 'cello back. Janet is our elder daughter, she's eleven and just started at the grammar school. Of all the instruments she had to choose to learn! I was all for hiring one from the school, which is a scheme they have, but Kate – typically – said we ought to give her one of her own. I got her this Japanese model, they're first-class actually, through contacts in the business. Unfortunately, her teacher reported that one of the peg things didn't fit properly and it seemed a pity not to start with it right.

Finding a parking bay was a problem, of course, which is why I may still have looked a little flustered. But one could hardly have borne it through the streets. In its case it's like a coffin; without the case one would risk stabbing passers-by with that lethal spike on the end! Anyway, I'm glad you enjoyed the cassata, it certainly looked appetizing.

What did we talk about? Do you know, I can hardly remember. I expect it will come back to me. For the moment I can think only of the way you laughed and looked around and sipped your wine and wanted to light a cigarette between courses – I didn't mind, honestly. And a certain teasing note in your voice when you talked about Geoffrey and asked me about Kate.

And that delightful habit, so unselfconscious that I'm sure you're not even aware of it, of adjusting yourself or, um, the cup or the strap or whatever, under your jumper. Though we're not in March yet I noticed you had only a thin blazer over it, even outdoors. I must challenge you sometime on your claim of never wearing a vest!

February 28

Oh, dear that garlic! I hope you didn't have any trouble. Kate made the most ridiculous fuss, which of course the children took up. She has this theory that it is exuded through the pores rather than just being borne on the breath. She also has an unreasonably developed sense of smell, if you ask me. 'What have you been eating?' she kept demanding. Luckily I had the Mugwumps business as an excuse for some celebration. Let's hope Kate doesn't happen to talk to Walter within the next day or two.

Anyway, the important thing is that I have at last told her about running into you, though I'm not sure if I carried it off well or not. Obviously it would have been much better to have come home with the news the day it actually happened. Also, I should have remembered about the 'cello.

How I broached the subject was to say at supper, as airily as I could. 'Guess who I bumped into,' without actually specifying, 'today'.

'Oh no, not him!' said Little Sam, and the girls groaned, because – I should have explained this first – we have this little fantasy about a Chief Sam who is in charge of all Little Sams and checks up regularly on their behaviour. I'm sure all parents have similar games. Kate will have invented it, she's very good at this sort of thing, but I go along with her by saying 'Guess who I saw coming our way in his big

17

yellow Rolls-Royce,' or 'Why, the Chief Sam was asking after you only yesterday!' Sam isn't *quite* sure that it's all pretend and likes to react very fiercely, shouting 'There's no such silly old Chief Sam.'

It very nearly put a stop to the whole ploy but by dint of saying several times through the din, 'No, it wasn't the Chief Sam,' I nudged Janet into saying, 'Well, go on then, Dad, you're dying to tell us.'

I took the plunge and said, 'Binnie Lines.'

There was a moment's silence and the most absurd chorus of chortles and whoops. *Wooo-wooo-wooo-woooo*, went Sam. It's the noise he applies to anything he considers salacious, such as seeing his sisters undressing or any suggestion of their having boy friends.

Miranda, little beast, cried, 'Dad's gone all red.'

'Dad*dy*,' I said as firmly as possible under the circumstances. I can't stand that uncouth 'Dad' they pick up at school. 'And anyway, I haven't. Don't talk nonsense.'

'You have, you have!'

Kate said, 'What a lovely surprise. You bumped into her, you say. Just like that?'

'It wouldn't be difficult,' said Janet. She gets it from her mother, I think, and though she can be very amusing there are times when she is too pert by half.

'Where 'bouts?' clamoured Miranda. 'Where was she?'

'There's no more to be said if everyone is going to be so silly.'

'Oh, come on,' said Kate. 'Share it with us. We like to hear about your adventures in the big city.'

'It wasn't, actually. It was on the train.'

'The train that goes to London?'

'That's right, Sam.'

Kate said, 'You didn't tell me you were going on the train today.'

I had to make a lightning decision. 'Oh, there was the

18

mother and father of all hold-ups on the motorway. The jam stretched all the way back to the roundabout. So I did a smart turn-about and went back to the station. Just got the 9.07—'

'Does that mean you didn't take my 'cello?' shrieked Janet.

'Of course I did.'

'On the train?'

'Why not? Nearly bayoneted the ticket-collector, mind you—'

'You took it out of its case?'

'Sssh, no, that was only a joke—'

'What's baytonid mean?'

'Hee-hee-hee-hee.'

Etcetera, etcetera, until Kate hushed them and said rather coldly, 'And she just happened to be in the same compartment?'

'Yes. Well, no. I mean, she was on the platform.'

'Here? At Prickwell.'

'I was about to say, that's the coincidence. They've come to live here. She and her husband, whatever his name is, and two children, I think. They were out in Tanganyika or somewhere. Of course, all that's gone by the board now. I gathered that he's never quite settled down to making a go of it back here. He's just joined S. C. Rimmer's in the personnel department. She was asking about schools and shops and the golf club and so on. I said that they must come over for a drink some time, and the children should get together – except theirs are away at school in term-time – and there were these coffee mornings you and your circle have. They've got a house in the Beechway. She was going in to have her hair done and see about some wallpaper. Apparently the previous people had the strangest tastes . . .'

I must try and overcome this habit I have of chattering

19

on when I'm nervous. I lost the attention of the table. Sam was muttering 'baytonid' to himself, he gets his words muddled rather amusingly at times. Janet had put on her sulky face and Miranda started saying 'He's gone red again.'

'Be quiet,' said Kate. 'Well that was nice for you, darling. I just wish you'd ask me before committing us all to bosom friendship with people we haven't met.'

Of course, 'bosom' set them all giggling again. I sometimes say, it's quite impossible to conduct a serious discussion on any topic whatsoever at our table. And anyway I hadn't committed anyone to anything. But Kate said no more except that she thought we'd agreed to put the Beechway behind us. She didn't mean this nastily, as I'll explain in a sec. It's simply that . . . well, Prickwell is a funny place. I mean, it's an awfully nice crowd of people. We first came nearly ten years ago when it was still quite a village. There were orchards where Barleymow Gardens are now, and a field with a horse in it behind Pipkin Lane, which is where we lived first. Even some of the old inhabitants lingered on: a very amusing old ruffian called Tom who'd been a poacher in his time, and a chap who actually kept pigs. And no supermarkets in the High Street in those days! Just an old-fashioned grocer's where you had your bacon sliced and your cheese weighed and your coffee beans ground. Old Colonel Chuter was just selling up at the Priory and moving down to Somerset. He'd been a kind of squire and chairman of the Preservation Society. Only when they'd thrown a big party and gone did everyone realize he'd sold off all the kitchen gardens and tennis court for development. That started quite a fashion – 'Divide and go', I called it. Divide off as much of the grounds as you could, you see, get planning permission and sell it to the builders. Then put the house itself on the market. The Coombes, the Richards, the ancient Lady Scores, they all followed suit. I must say I had expected a little less selfishness from people of their sort.

It's true that we sold a little plot in Pipkin Lane just before we moved, there's a bungalow there now, but that was quite different. It was simply an idea of Kate's that we ought to think about her parents' – or my parents' – old age and one day, perhaps, install them in a 'granny annexe'. So I applied for planning permission more as a long-term precaution than anything else . . .

Anyway, all these new houses were being built, and a new class of person moving in. 'Young executives', they were supposed to be, according to the property ads. 'A select development of executive-type dwellings.' Here, I hope I'm not saying anything out of turn. I suppose Geoffrey is an executive! – come to that, we're all executives, even my next-door neighbour Max, who's an executive in the army. It's just that, well, one began to have the impression of a rather *faster* life-style going on around one. You know, flashy cars and drinks out on the patio and some parties we were invited to that were distinctly free and easy. There were rumours of even less inhibited ones. Actually the Beechway had rather a special reputation in this respect! It was one particular crowd who set the pace, the Merrills and the Fox-Rogerses. I'm sure it's all quite different now.

Mind you, Prickwell itself has always had a certain reputation among car salesmen and people like that. It's the name, of course, especially as we're not far from Maidenhead! You must have heard all the so-called witticisms. Actually, it's nothing to do with a well, either. I always tell our visitors that the derivation is from the Anglo-Saxon *prician* and *wealden*, meaning a wood or forest shaped like a goad.

Or, according to the Vicar, where they found the very hard thorns they used as goads.

At all events, when we heard about this house out on the heath coming onto the market Kate pushed me to try for it. She's always had rather grand ideas of how she wants to live, although between you and me her background is perfectly ordinary. Her father ran a country hotel, as a matter of fact. I must say it is nice to be so far from the madding crowd. Do you know the heath yet? There are these two properties over in the north-east corner, nothing else for half a mile in either direction, just the Kennerlys and us. But I needn't waste time describing it. You'll be able to see for yourself, I hope.

At least the ground is now clear.

Chapter Two

Wondered if you might be at morning service yesterday, but I surmise that you and Geoffrey are not churchgoers. Why should you be? Frankly, it is Kate who is the moving spirit in our family. She believes the children should have the benefit of the traditional upbringing which as a hotel child she feels she missed. Also it was impressed upon us by old Colonel Chuter when we first moved to Prickwell that it was up to people like us to support the institution which was so much a part of village life, even if one didn't go along with all the mumbo-jumbo, what?!

Certainly I like to keep an open mind on questions of actual faith, etcetera. It is perfectly possible to enjoy the singing and the pageantry without necessarily affixing one's name to the 39 Articles! Not that pageantry is much in Father Lumsden's style – typically, he objects to being thus addressed, preferring 'Mister' or even the ignorant 'Reverend'. He is very low-church and more than a little 'Red', judging by his sermons. Quite a few we know have deserted his flock for Pinkney Dene, which is the pretty little country church you may have noticed out on the Browsden road. But I say there is such a thing as loyalty.

23

Did I tell you about this idea I had for a model Vicar Walter and I might get out? On the lines of the *Action Man* figures with all those outfits and accoutrements a boy can collect – such good psychology! Just the thing that would have appealed to me at age eleven or so. I can remember making charts of all the wartime medal ribbons with coloured pencils. It struck me that the bits and pieces of a vicar's wardrobe would have some of the attraction, besides being educational in the best sense. There are the different coloured vestments for the different seasons of the year. Then one might make him a service chaplain – the title *Action Padre* crossed my mind, in point of fact. He could have different uniforms plus a parachute for going in with the airborne troops, and one of those field communion kits one reads of. I must ask Max for details.

March 4

Only a brief word tonight as I gave Max Kennerly a lift in this morning and promised to pick him up from Earls Court again this evening, whereby hangs a silly story. It's so irritating I'd rather just try and forget it, but for the record – as they say – what happened was that one of their boys at public school was hit in the eye playing hockey and Sue Kennerly wanted to take their car and drive up to Oundle there and then. She'd stay overnight and then see how he was. Max clearly thought she was being too fussy but you're a mother yourself, I expect you're just as soft about your children. Kate certainly is.

Anyway, when he popped his head in last night to make arrangements he was very solicitous that I shouldn't be put out at all: if I were planning to go by train, a lift to the station would be just as welcome. I said no, I mostly preferred to drive up these days and of course Kate had to bring up the exception, like the other day when the motorway had been

24

so choked I'd returned to the station. Max started asking questions as to exactly what time and where – I suppose it's the military mind, must get everything tabulated. Absurdly, I felt myself going quite red again.

Later, quite out of the blue Kate said, 'Was it with *her* you had that garlicky lunch?'

'Of course not,' I retorted, though thinking it over now I realize I should have said, 'Who?' or 'What on earth are you talking about?'

It really is ridiculous that one should be made to feel guilty without any reason. I only want us all to become friends.

March 5

Waiting for Max at Empress State building last night I had a brainwave. A little dinner party for you and Geoffrey and him and Sue might have just the *raison d'être* that would appeal to Kate. She loves bringing people together who turn out to have something in common. We once had two couples both called David and Meg. 'David and Meg, meet David and Meg.' They got on jolly well together, too. Now you and Geoffrey were in Africa and so, I'm sure, were Max and Sue. They've been everywhere like that. Plus the fact that you were both in government service – he's in the army, a Brigadier actually. I must confess that when we were in the process of moving to the heath and heard there was a Colonel next door – as he was then – my heart sank. Imagined some red-faced old buffer like Colonel Chuter. Kate, I think, was more chuffed. She was brought up in rather colonely country, as she puts it.

As it happened, the place was empty until after we'd been in several weeks. They were still out in Singapore or somewhere. Sue arrived first, in time for the school holidays, and that was the first surprise – you know, very sweet

25

and friendly and young. Max followed and of course he turned out to be no more than forty-five and absolutely un-colonely. We've never seen him in uniform! I suppose he must have one. He speaks very softly except sometimes to Miles and Pete, their two boys. By the way, the one that was hit in the eye, Pete, is quite all right. There's also a girl, Sarah. Or if you're at all indecisive when trying to plan something with him you might just notice a slightly peremptory note to his voice.

Guess what he likes doing best? Playing the piano. If the windows are open in summer we sometimes hear him for hours on end. Beethoven and Chopin and some strange plonking music that's not quite up my street though Kate says she likes it. She plays well herself – did I tell you? But she reckons Max could have been on the concert platform if he'd put his mind to it.

Instead he travels into town every day like any other commuter and sits at a desk in the Ministry of Defence.

He's rather witty, too. When we first went next door for a drink and Sue Kennerly introduced us, 'Max, this is Kate and Graham Godley' he said, 'Well, now Kennerliness really is next to Godliness.' I thought that was awfully neat unless, of course, he'd worked it out in advance.

March 6

You got in first! I was flabbergasted when I walked into the kitchen and Kate greeted me in her direct fashion with 'Your friend has been on the phone,' and when I looked genuinely puzzled, 'Binnie Lines – or Binnie Davies as she is now.'

'Oh, yes,' I said non-committally. You can imagine how my mind was racing! 'I wonder where she got the number from.'

'Well, it is in the book,' said Kate. 'Can we go to a party

tomorrow, it's all on the spur of the moment, nothing elaborate, it's just that they felt it was time they had a few neighbours in. Oh, and would we take a bottle!'

I didn't know what to say. I mean, I've mentioned Kate's slight snobbishness – I'm afraid there's no other word for it – about the Beechway and Beechway people, as she calls them. Plus this silly attitude towards you. Plus the fact that we did agree we'd never go to another bottle party. There were rather a lot of them when we were in Pipkin Lane and as Kate said at the time, if people can't afford to entertain they shouldn't. I'm sure it's quite different in your case, merely following the custom of the country. And if you take your own bottle at least you know what's in it! We were nearly poisoned once or twice by people who served things like champagne cocktails, only made of Spanish brandy and that fizzy apple stuff.

So I said, 'I don't mind. Whatever you like.'

'We'd better go, then.'

After fourteen years there are still times when I have no idea how Kate is going to jump. She never mentioned the subject again all evening, except to wonder about a baby-sitter. Fortunately the Kennerly girl is home at the moment. I dare say there'll be a few sighs tonight when it's time to change and set out. Half of me is looking forward to it, the other half is a mass of nerves!

March 10

Now please don't worry about my suit. It wasn't an expensive one – it's simply not worth spending a fortune on clothes when one can find such excellent 'ready to wear' these days. Anyway, it can go to the cleaners. There is always a life and soul of the party like that Patrick whatever-his-name-was, and it was my own fault for allowing myself to be drawn into his silly games. I gather he

27

was one of those young chaps who went into the services and then opted for the silver bowler after a few years. I suppose they get up to that sort of horseplay in the mess, though I cannot imagine Max Kennerly enjoying it very much.

I was afraid Kate would be rather scathing, but on the way home she seemed to find it more amusing than anything. 'At least it makes a change from hovering in the corner with a ghastly smile,' she said.

'What on earth do you mean?'

'Dancing with that Mollie Fox-Rogers.'

'For old times' sake, that's all.'

'The Bossa Nova into the bargain.'

'Is that what it was?'

'Telling loud stories about the Mugwumps and Zillah Graves.'

'People like a bit of behind-the-scenes gossip.'

'Playing that foolish game. What got into you? Poo – it would have to be garlic again.'

'For heaven's sake, not so very long ago we were going to parties like that every week.'

'With you blindfolded and trying to balance a bowl of avocado dip on your head?' Then she relapsed into rather exaggerated chortlings, I thought. I was afraid the story would be trotted out next day and taken up by the children and endlessly embroidered throughout the weekend but luckily – I don't mean this unkindly, of course – she had this headache and upset tum and stayed in bed for most of Saturday. Personally I feel fine and I'm sure that Geoffrey's delicious cider cup had nothing to do with it. It was probably one of the bottles that people bring along, or all those drinks the golf club contingent were trying to give her.

Do you know, I think she rather enjoyed herself! As I said before, she has acquired this rather superior attitude to the Beechway and I was a little apprehensive. I should have remembered that she has a great gift for socializing and of course there were plenty of people we knew from our Pipkin Lane days. I was so pleased, though also a little jealous to see her the centre of attention – that is, when you were not yourself occupying that place! I must say you looked quite stunning. Kate *was* a little critical about your dress as she can't go in for very low neck-lines herself, she always says. I'm sure she's much too sensitive in this respect. Not everyone can be Junoesque, if that's the phrase. In fact there was one girl I couldn't help noticing, the tall fair one with the sort of silky jacket that was only fastened in one place, who looked most alluring though she had only a very boyish figure.

With so many attractive ladies around, no wonder I felt the need to be more competitive than usual! Hence the ridiculous business with the avocado dip. It was awfully sweet of you to say straightaway that it didn't matter about the carpet, though I don't blame Geoffrey for being a little put out. I would have been the same. I thought he was a very interesting person, especially as regards a certain sardonic note I detected in things he said. There was someone who must also work for S. C. Rimmer's going on about how good a firm they are. 'Just like one big family,' he said, and Geoffrey replied drily, 'That's the trouble.' The other fellow looked quite shocked.

I'm sorry I couldn't quite enter into the spirit of his 'gambling hell'. He really had set this up very professionally in that other room, with the roulette wheel and the proper shoe for the cards in baccarat. Believe it or not Walter and I once tried to bring out a kiddies' version of this game under the name *Take a Card*, but it didn't catch on.

Unfortunately I don't have much of a gambling instinct. Besides, there seemed to be plenty of others anxious to join in. Certainly it will have been something of an innovation for Prickwell, where the gayer parties are more often associated with, well, what I fear was going on without your quite realizing it. When I went upstairs to try and clean off the worst of the avocado dip I had to step over several couples, while in the spare room, it must have been – I pushed open the door mistaking it for the bathroom – the most abandoned scene met my eyes. It was that Audrey creature whom we know of old, though who the two men were I'm not sure.

I did like your bathroom. I always think that nothing tells one more about a woman than her dressing-table or her bathroom. The thick carpet on the floor, the pink suite, the gold taps, all those bottles of bath salts and eau de cologne and perfume – I can imagine you at your leisurely toilet. Not in any prying way, I hasten to add: I'm not like that, thank goodness. It was kind of you to pop up and offer to sponge my trousers if I would take them off but Kate might not have appreciated the gesture! I do hope you and she will be friends. You seemed to be getting on well enough, the times I saw you together, and as I said, I really think she enjoyed herself. Apart from anything else I suspect that she takes pleasure in going back to the Beechway and feeling that she has now risen above it. Oh dear, that makes me sound even snobbier, not to mention disloyal to Kate. By the way, she was perfectly well again by Sunday.

Did you register what I murmured to you on the landing? There is this rather quaint little pub across the other side of the heath. Actually it was an ale-house until a few weeks ago, which meant it only sold beer and catered mainly for the estate workers and suchlike from Browsden and Pinkney Dene. There was just the one dingy room and a place like a scullery at the back where the old boy or his crone would draw the beer straight from the barrel. Not exactly the last word in hygiene, and of course no place to take a lady, which always seemed a pity as it would have been so handy for us. I went with Max Kennerly once or twice, that's all. He professed to like the place. Anyway, it's now been taken over by a very nice chap who already has a place on the river below Browsden, and completely done up inside – you wouldn't recognize it – and renamed it the Browsden Arms. What's more he's added some delightful light luncheon dishes one can enjoy with a glass of wine, not just the usual sausages and rolls but things like *quiche lorraine* and scampi in the basket.

At the weekend it's already getting very crowded. Luckily it's still quiet during the week. The point I'm coming to is that every so often I take a day or two at home to re-charge the batteries as Walter puts it, and do a bit of quiet thinking and working out of ideas – and with the books going ahead again I shall really need to get down to some solid brain-work! If Kate is doing Meals-on-Wheels, as she does on Mondays and Wednesdays now that Little Sam is having school dinners at last, Wednesdays I sometimes saunter across for a bite and a glass of plonk for my lunch. Take Rastus with me for the run and I've killed two birds with one stone.

It occurs to me that you might be able to meet me there if you've nothing better to do. And for once I wouldn't have to go back to the office immediately afterwards!

March 20

Kate always says that autumn is her favourite season on the heath, with the trees turning and a mistiness in the air. But I think the fresh green leaves and buds of spring are just as pretty and much more forward-looking if you see what I mean. Life is stirring. It's a time to be alive and young, and my goodness I feel alive and young after such a nice day as yesterday.

I'm glad you liked the pub. You can't imagine how it looked before Charles took it over. He was awfully pleas-ant, wasn't he? Could tell he was smitten by you, but he's

31

the soul of discretion. Says he had no option but to become so, running that place on the river!

And hardly anyone else there, though I have to say I was a bit startled by that couple who were just leaving. I didn't say anything at the time and actually I doubt if she recognized me, so wrapped up was she in that awful long-haired yob, but the girl was the Kennerlys' daughter, Sarah. She's supposed to be a student at one of these new universities, Essex or East Anglia or wherever it is they're always agitating. She brings some dreadful specimen home with her every vacation. Secretly, I imagine, Max and Sue must be very worried, though they always pretend to be pleased with her.

It was fun talking over the party. I'm relieved the carpet cleaned up satisfactorily, and I must say you seem to have wasted no time in weighing up your fellow denizens of the Beechway! Personally I think those stories about wife-exchanging and so on are quite exaggerated, but there is no doubt the Merrils and Co. have a strange notion of their marriage vows. I was most amused by your speculation on the practical difficulties of conducting an *affaire* these days, despite all the talk of a 'permissive society'. For your friend in London, as you said, there was simply no place to go with her lover: both of them married with children and *au pair* girls in the house even if the spouse should be absent, and it still requiring a certain amount of defiance to go to a hotel in the middle of the day!

As for going away for the weekend, as they do in books and films – well, as you pointed out, it must be awfully tricky to think of convincing excuses to go off to strange hotels by oneself. Normally one stays with friends, which is what you're planning to do in Scotland next month, I think you said. And even if one were at a hotel one's husband would expect to know which hotel, and to ring one up there. It's really much easier to stick to the straight and narrow.

By the way, I'm sorry I happened to telephone when you were in the bath, but it seemed a good opportunity while Kate was in the utility room getting the wash into the washing-machine and wouldn't want to be ringing any of her friends, etcetera. So you have your tub every morning about this time? I remarked that another day I must call with my message personally, and when you just joked back 'Why not?' my heart gave quite a little bump. Silly, of course.

It was the same when I challenged you about never wearing a vest and you whipped up the hem of your jumper and exposed several inches of bare midriff. I must say you have the firmest, smoothest skin. And still tanned in March. I wasn't surprised to hear you and Geoffrey have a sun-lamp. Kate and I both have rather fair complexions and have to be careful not to peel, but again I might drop in at the Beechway some time for a spot of sunshine!

It was such an artless, unselfconscious little gesture. Quite disturbing, really.

Dear old Rastus enjoyed the outing as much as I did. I tend to agree with you about pets and if I had my way we'd have none either. But the children have had a lot of fun from him and Poggles the cat and Miranda's rabbit and Sam's guinea-pig, and perhaps learned a little compassion towards less fortunate species. I just wish Sam wouldn't put his face so close to them all, that's all. And much as I complain about having to take Rastus out for runs on the heath it does give me a bit of fresh air and exercise I might otherwise avoid!

Considering he's only a cross-breed, I think you must agree he was no trouble at all in the pub, curling up under the table and not begging for food. We've brought him up very strictly in such matters.

And how he rushed about, retrieving sticks and pretending to flush pheasants, on our little walk afterwards.

Actually he did catch a pheasant once, over towards Browsden. It was very amusing to see the luckless bird flying along about two feet above the ground and Rastus running behind him, firmly attached to his long tail. Of course he got away a moment later and Rasty was left with only a mouthful of feathers. I wondered if Max might be keen on shooting, being in the army, and perhaps introduce me to the sport, but apart from music his only hobby seems to be sailing. In that respect he resembles a certain politician we both know!

Yes, that was his house to the right of ours. You could just pick out the chimneys. I'm sorry we didn't venture nearer but I hadn't realized you had been hoping to see where we live. It might have been a little tactless if Kate had just been returning from Meals-on-Wheels. In any case it was one of Mrs Wild's cleaning mornings. You'll see it when you come to dinner.

And all too soon it was time for you to retrieve your little Fiat and wend your way home. I'm sorry to hear it's giving you a bit of trouble starting. With only two cylinders, of course, one has to keep the points up to scratch. I'm kicking myself for not telling you about Dino. He's a marvellous mechanic, especially with Fiats, of course, being an Italian. At least he was originally – a P.o.W. here who stayed on. He's still got an accent but it's all mixed with bits of Berkshire and Buckinghamshire and Slough, which itself is a mixture; the result is the strangest hotch-potch you ever heard, quite incomprehensible and judging by some of the adjectives one does detect, just as well!

He has that little yard just behind the row of cottages they're going to pull down in Kiln Lane. The last of the old Prickwell, in some ways, I suppose, and a real rural slum. There are engines rusting away among the nettles, and hens laying in the back seats of an old Buick, and an enormous walnut tree that scatters walnuts everywhere in the autumn. But if you can persuade Dino to take you on, and he's very choosy, I can tell you, he'll keep any car in sparkling form. He's got real 'black fingers' as I always put it.

The more I think about it, the surer I am that the Kennerly girl didn't see me. She'd have said something.

I might drop by tomorrow to tell you about Dino.

March 26

Well, after three days I'm just beginning to see the humorous side but I don't mind admitting I spent the weekend in a terrible state of nerves for fear some repercussion might reach our neck of the woods. Repercussion! – one can say that again. The sound of that dustbin is still crashing in my ears. 'What *is* the matter?' said Kate. 'I thought that Mugwumps business had all been settled.' I pretended there was a fresh worry in connection with a change in command in Children's Programmes at the BBC, which is in fact the case.

Also Rastus will keep on cringing if I try to make a fuss of him. I accept full responsibility for having brought him with me. I know how you feel about animals. It's simply that it seems so much more natural to have a dog when one is going for a walk, the more so when it is a walk of two or three miles and in the rain. Yes, I could have pretended to be fetching something from the shops and taken the car, but somehow that would have been too . . . calculated.

Not that there was anything underhand about the expedition. I really do find that a long walk is often more productive of clear thinking than sitting huddled over a desk, especially after a substantial breakfast! Moreover I was anxious to put you on to Dino before you took your little Fiat all the way to Maidenhead or somewhere to be serviced. So as soon as Kate had left to do her big weekend shop, off we set; across the heath, down Long Lane – and it

35

really is a long lane when one is on foot – and past the golf course. Rastus bounded ahead and I was striding out.

Unfortunately the rain came on rather heavily by the time we reached the council depot and I had rashly forgotten to bring any sort of hat. Caps don't suit me and the other sorts are so staid, I always think. Then in Boundary Road, of course, I had to put Rastus on the lead. They are really very fussy about that new by-law; little notices all over the place. I expect you agree with it, but some dogs just won't perform whilst on the lead, if you know what I mean.

Finally we gained the Beechway, all very nice and quiet. I thought it a reasonable assumption that quite a few of the ladies would also be shopping, or off to bring-and-buys etcetera. Hoped you weren't! Then there was your little Fiat standing in the drive in the rain – I remember you explaining, ruefully, that the garage was still full of furniture and tea-chests, etcetera, from abroad.

Thought it better not to ring the bell as it was about the time you said you took a bath, and nothing is more annoying than having to don a wrap and come down and answer the door. I could easily call up to you and wait below.

So I went straight to the back door, though of course it's actually at the side of your house, and looked for somewhere to tie Rastus up. I admit that the dustbin wasn't the cleverest solution but it seemed very solid and it did have these convenient little handles on the sides. If there'd been a gate separating the back of the property from the front everything would have been perfectly all right. I never did like this American-style open layout, it doesn't suit our national character.

Just at that moment the drainpipe started to gush the most deliciously fragrant, steaming water. I let myself in and tip-toed through the kitchen and just went a little way up the stairs, so that you'd hear me above the gurgle of the emptying bath. As soon as I saw the bathroom door was half open I stopped, I assure you.

That's when you would have heard me call, 'Binnie' and then again, a little more loudly, 'Binnie!'

'Who is it?' you shrieked.

Well, of course it must have been a bit alarming, which is why I came up another couple of steps to make sure you'd hear me call, 'Graham! Graham Godley!' But by that time you'd slammed the door shut. There wasn't any need, honestly. I'm not like that. Besides, everywhere was full of steam.

Anyway, we sorted out our identities. I suppose it must have sounded odd, my announcing that I just wanted to tell you where to take the Fiat! I heard you laugh and then the door opened an inch or two and you said you would be down in a jiffy.

I was so relieved that I all but missed you as you scampered across the landing wrapped in a big towel and giving me such a lovely smile! In fact you were jolly sporting about the whole thing. What was that heady fragrance, I wonder? Some sort of bath stuff? Incidentally, I'm sorry about dripping on to the stair carpet. That's the trouble with PVC, the rain just runs off it. It shouldn't have stained, though.

I was just debating with myself whether I should climb the rest of the stairs and converse with you through the bedroom door when that horrific racket started up outside, a yelping and crashing and banging to rouse the entire neighbourhood. Obviously what happened was that Rastus spied a cat – as you said, doubtless the Merrills' wretched Siamese at The Hirsel, as they're pleased to call their perfectly ordinary house. Whereupon he gave chase, pulled the dustbin over and the clatter so frightened him that he dragged it into the road and right along to where he got it tangled round the lamp post. I knew he was quite a strong dog but had no idea he was as strong as that!

37

Admittedly, it would have got lighter as the contents spilled out.

I must confess my immediate fear was that people would jump to the conclusion that it was a deliberate and cruel prank. The prospect of being reported to the RSPCA stared me in the face. But as soon as I had Rastus calmed down a little I turned my attention to the mess in the road, which is when you arrived on the scene. I was so distraught that I could only shake my head. Then you started to laugh. For a moment I feared it must be hysteria, then I saw it was real, helpless laughter. What a relief! As I said, I can't imagine anyone else behaving so sportingly.

What a pair we must have looked, I with my hair plastered down by the rain, you with yours still wet from the bath and convulsed with merriment! Not that you weren't also disturbingly attractive. I dare say you had nothing on under that shiny yellow macintosh. And just slippers on your feet.

Anyway, we got it all back into the bin. I'm glad I insisted on picking up the less savoury items such as the potato peelings and used tea-bags and that chicken carcase while you fetched a dustpan and brush to deal with the broken wine bottles. That little paper bag that disintegrated in my hand was rather an unpleasant experience, mind you! Kate always uses the giblets for the gravy and afterwards the cat has them, so there are no disposal problems for us.

The extraordinary thing is that no one came out from the other houses, though I'm sure I felt a dozen pairs of eyes on me. Perhaps we were in luck. Or are you by now being made only too aware that there were witnesses? I wish I knew.

It was sweet of you to offer to drive us back, but the walk helped Rastus to recover some more and I managed to scrub the worst of the smell off my hands whilst ostensibly drying his paws in the outhouse. Sometimes I fancy there's still a whiff of it on me, though. And sometimes I catch, too, a mysterious trace of the fragrance that spilled from your bathroom.

Chapter Three

A week gone by and no tales seemed to have reached Kate. Indeed she has been at her serenest, and of course has now arranged the little dinner to which you and Geoffrey will be coming. It gave me quite an odd feeling to hear her telephoning you with the invitation. I wonder what you said to each other. From her manner and that little laugh she gave once or twice the atmosphere seemed most cordial. The happiest aspect of all is that she took the initiative. I had been careful not to mention your name again once our 'post-mortems' on your party were over. I have often noticed with Kate that once she can entertain anyone I want her to like this rather suspicious side to her nature completely vanishes.

Max and Sue Kennerly are also invited, just as I had hoped.

But now we seem to have escaped any embarrassing consequences of the little episode with the dustbin, anxiety has been replaced by . . . well, I can't help wishing things could have turned out more romantically. A cup of coffee together in the kitchen, your hair damp from the bath, your feet in slippers, pleasant music coming softly from the radio

40

– what a delightful picture of stolen pleasures I conjure up!

Don't misunderstand me. It is simply that ever since I was a child I've especially enjoyed any little treat that was also rather a secret, like being surreptitiously let off games at school in order to tidy the miniature range, things like that. When I did National Service there was this dreadful training camp, I hated every minute. But sometimes if it was just a small detail of us out on some errand or another, the corporal would march us down a side-street and into the local bakehouse where for a few coppers we were allowed to buy a mug of coffee and a doughnut still warm from the oven. Because it was unofficial it was all the more delicious.

As I've made clear all along, Kate and I are very happy and ideally suited. It is a fact that I am very unlucky as regards any raffle or tombola, etcetera, that comes our way. Nor have any of our Premium Bonds ever paid out. But I always say that in one lottery I've drawn the top prize, and that's the lottery of marriage!

We share all that life brings us, the good and the bad, the triumphs and the disasters, the grey days and the sunny days – and we have had our ups and downs, I don't mind saying. I am sure it's the same with you and Geoffrey. At the same time one does feel an occasional need to enjoy some quite private experience, to keep some innocent little secret to oneself. I must ask if you feel the same. Reflecting on that amusing conversation we had at the Browsden Arms, I wonder if this aspect of infidelity does not represent a great deal of the attraction?

Perhaps it would be possible to enjoy the conspiracy without, of course, committing oneself to the actual deception?

Honestly, on balance I count it a perfectly enjoyable evening – if not one of our little dinners to earn a subsequent
alpha in the Habitat engagement calendar we hang in the
kitchen, a perfectly respectable Beta-minus. I admit I saw
no need for Kate to have invited the Vicar on top of
everyone else and then, since he is unmarried, have been
obliged to make up numbers with the Kennerly girl. Phew!
Thank goodness she didn't give anything away, though
from the way she kept staring I felt sure that she was going
to recognize you from the pub and blurt out some tactless
remark. Also, it must be said that 'Reverend' Lumsden is
not the most affable of churchmen. But given this handicap
I thought the 'mix' was quite a successful one.

Politics were bound to intrude, I suppose. How interesting that Geoffrey and Max should be on opposite sides but
not in the way one would expect! For some reason, perhaps
his sardonic remark about S. C. Rimmer's at your party, I
had assumed that Geoffrey was a 'progressive'. I should
have remembered that coming back to Britain after fifteen
years abroad would be somewhat disillusioning in all sorts
of ways, especially to one who has been in government
service. By the way I only introduced the word 'empire-
builder' in an effort to head off the Kennerly girl and her
mutterings about 'imperialism'. It certainly wasn't
intended to be provocative – I say a good host's first
requirement is to keep the balance and soothe any feathers
that may be ruffled. I can certainly understand Geoffrey's
bitterness. 'Empire dismantler, you mean,' he said vehem-
ently. Not only to lose a career in mid-life but also see
everything you've built handed over to some African who
gets the job simply because he is an African – it would be a
difficult adjustment for anyone to make.

Many of Max's liberal sentiments, of course, were

already familiar to me, though I've never been quite sure how genuine he is in this respect and how much of it can be put down to this role of the rather unconventional army officer which he clearly enjoys playing. Did you notice how dismissive he was of his duties at the Ministry of Defence and preferred only to talk about the street market he's discovered in Fulham? A brigadier going shopping with a string bag in his lunch hour! He went on quite absurdly about those fresh limes he'd found. And the long lecture about the fish stall in Slough Market! It *is* good, Kate tells me, but I'm sure one can find there plenty of perfectly good fish from around our own shores without the need to rhapsodize about these Caribbean varieties which are imported for the benefit of the West Indians.

Perhaps it is a taste he acquired out there. I hadn't realized they had been stationed in those parts at one time. I suppose one's views of colonial life are bound to be coloured by whichever colony you know best, and I know from other conversations we've had that Max was sincerely disturbed by some of the extremes of poverty and wealth he observed abroad. Oh dear, I'm making him sound rather a 'trendy' which he manifestly is not. It is just that he does also have a habit of putting on an attitude which isn't really his own, purely to keep the argument going! Underneath the banter his values are as sound as anyone's. I hope Geoffrey noticed that Max was the first to admit that self-government had often failed to produce any benefits for the people. Quite the contrary, in fact.

As for state education versus private, that was Kate, I fear, leading the dance! Max has the grace to admit that he can hardly argue against fee-paying schools when all his children go – or did go – to boarding school, though Sue is always quick to point out that with their being shuttled around the world they had no choice. Twenty homes in twenty years, she said, if you remember. By the time they finally settled here even the younger boy was already launched upon the fee-paying system. Not that it's done much for the girl, as you'll have seen for yourselves. Another term at that university of hers and she'll be indistinguishable from any product of the secondary modern! Both the boys, I must tell you, are charming and respectful.

Kate's passionate belief in state schools has always rather surprised me. She's hardly a Socialist in other respects, though I've often envied the ease with which she seems to get on with people from all walks of life. I suspect it may be a reaction to the rather snobbish 'county' set in which she grew up without ever really belonging. Her father's hotel was patronized by the hunting crowd, and when she was a teenager the young bloods would take her out. She had an Hon. who was very keen! But I gather that sooner or later she was always reminded that her people were in trade.

None of which excuses her rather sweeping dismissal of your defence of your boarding school. I'm afraid that when she's riding her favourite hobby-horse she can be a little overbearing. Mind you, that old fool Lumsden didn't help. I shouldn't speak so of the cloth, I know, but it was no business of his to take her side against you. Easy for him, not having any children of his own. Personally, I am of the same opinion as yourself: people should be quite free to choose the education they want for their children. Janet is doing well at the grammar school and I shall be perfectly happy for Miranda to follow her there providing she passes her eleven-plus. Luckily they're dragging their feet in this county as regards all that comprehensives nonsense. Then one would hope to be able to have them 'finished', to use the old-fashioned term, in order to smooth off the rough edges and do something about their accents and the table manners – or lack of them – they pick up at school dinners.

In the case of Little Sam, though, my mind is already more than half made up to send him away. Apart from being one's son and heir and as a boy *needing* the best possible start it is clear even from junior infant school that he has neither Janet's industry nor Miranda's quickness. They make the best of the state system, he is likely to make the worst! I haven't discussed it with Kate yet, and I know there will be ructions. Nevertheless I've already started to investigate prep schools. Then at thirteen, all being well, he shall go to whichever public school suggests itself. I dare say Max would help with Oundle if that's where the choice fell.

Oh, I can hear you objecting that girls are just as important. So they are! So they are! And if one could have afforded it, one wouldn't have hesitated. Unfortunately there wasn't a lot of money about at the time, especially when Walter and I first set up on our own; never even enough to pay into one of those insurance schemes. And neither granny and grandpa were in a position to help.

At least we were united in deploring what the builders have done to Prickwell, though again old Lumsden couldn't resist a dig at someone, i.e. me. Did you notice? – that reference to 'cramped little bungalows'. I'm sure he was alluding to the plot we sold in Pipkin Lane, which as I've explained arose simply from an abortive plan to house Kate's parents. He is hardly in a position to talk, having disposed of the beautiful rambling old vicarage and all its grounds for development into what is Vicarage Gate. Of course the proceeds didn't go to him personally but part of the deal with Smailes – he's the demon despoiler round these parts, as no doubt you're aware – was that garish new split-level vicarage. Have you seen it? Looks more like a roadhouse than the offical residence of a man of God. In any case, what need has an old bachelor of double garage, fitted kitchen and a sunken bath, or so we're told? One might also wonder as to the exact function of that young fellow he has living in. His 'house-boy' he calls him. I gather he has seen the inside of more than one Borstal.

Incidentally, I hope you won't think Kate was trying to show off with all those references to the books Walter and I are planning. Of course, mention of *Stanley the Suburban Squirrel* did arise perfectly naturally from the conversation about builders – the villain is going to be just such an arch-enemy as Smailes! But I sometimes feel Kate places too much emphasis on what will only be a small part of our business, at least to begin with. I expect the idea of being a publisher's lady appeals to her. Personally, I am quite content to be what I am. Toys and games are every bit as important to the growing mind as books.

Apropos of which, one might have expected a less sarcastic response to my *Action Padre* idea from Lumsden. After all, it is the church that would benefit from a legion of small boys grown up with the idea of the man of God as a hero. To tell the truth, the incident has led me to decide finally to transfer our worship to Pinkney Dene, which is run by a very pleasant chap with a young family. I'm only waiting for my Christian stewardship covenant to run out in July and we're off. I mean, it would be silly to be giving to two churches at the same time.

It was good of Geoffrey to come to my rescue. Underneath those bantering remarks of his one could see that he was genuinely impressed by the idea. That was a valuable suggestion he made about marketing different denominations, e.g. Catholic, C. of E. and perhaps Jewish, providing the little customers weren't encouraged to mix up the various accessories too ecumenically!

Motorway exit coming up and I've been rambling on about the small talk of a dinner party for half an hour or more.

Resolutely, dearest Binnie, resolutely.

Trying so hard not to dwell on a fleeting moment, or to read too much into a fleeting touch.

But I'm not dreaming, am I? When Kate said you must

see round the house, for she loves to show it off, and you and I came down the steep little stair from the girls' landing ahead of the others, did I or did I not take your hand? As I fumbled for the light switch in the playroom it remained in mine, didn't it, warm and soft and vibrant? And when I lightly kissed you, you only broke away with a little laugh and a last squeeze of my hand when we heard their footsteps above.

Down to earth again in the kitchen when that foolish Rastus cringed away from you! I don't mind saying it gave me a slight turn, as if everyone were bound to divine the business with the dustbin that time. Ridiculous of me, I know. But you did laugh rather guiltily and Geoffrey didn't help, saying so loudly that he thought animals were supposed to like you. Never mind, it all blew over. Now I only want to see you again. Do you have to go to that friend in Scotland?

April 11

How nice of you to ring with your thanks. Kate appreciated it very much. She prefers to drop a little note herself but I think that's rather formal in this day and age, especially between people living reasonably close to each other. Now they've closed the sorting office in Prickwell it means the letter has to go all the way to Maidenhead, then come back virtually to where it started from. At least we still have our own telephone exchange.

By the way, I'm sorry if I disconcerted you by blurting out somewhat intimate proposals etcetera when I took the call. From your reactions I deduced that Geoffrey might be in earshot and hastily amended my conversation to details of the date I have made with Dino for your little car. What I had just thought of and hoped to put to you was the following idea: you are going up to stay with your friend in

Helensburgh. Jessie Blair, you said. On reflection I think I do remember her now. Wasn't she one of your hand-maidens when you were Charities Queen? Red hair and rather thick legs? Anyway, it so happens that there is a Toy Fair in Glasgow which I thought of visiting. It is only a hotel show, not one of the big events like Brighton or Harrogate, but no renewal of dealer contacts is entirely valueless. If Walter was rather surprised at the suggestion he made no serious objection!

Normally one would fly or take the sleeper, but at this time of year it might be rather pleasant to drive up together. We need not kill ourselves battling up the M.6 in one day. I thought of breaking the journey in the Lake District. Of course, our respective spouses might well misconstrue that part of the scheme, so it would perhaps be just as well to keep the travel arrangements to ourselves. You could tell Geoffrey you fancied a little adventure and were going to toddle up in the Fiat, and then garage it somewhere. Or if he preferred to think of you going by train I could pick you up in London.

Anyway, I will put all this to you when I see you.

April 14

Yes, I do realize that the car journey would have been impracticable. As you pointed out so forcibly, I would look askance at any proposal of Kate's to drive four hundred miles in a baby Fiat, and four hundred back, simply for a few days stay in Glasgow. Why should I suppose Geoffrey to be any more complaisant? As for pretences of going by rail while actually going by road, the risks are obvious. Supposing he were to telephone Jessie to make sure you'd arrived safely!

But the very fact that you were objecting only to means and not to the proposition itself is exciting. I just wish we could have had enough time to go properly into possible alternatives. I had rather counted on a few minutes chat and a cup of coffee, perhaps, after we had deposited the car. But, as you say, the children come first. With them away at school so much, one forgets you have them on your hands in the holidays. Meanwhile I will certainly look into the sleeper idea. As you say, it has certain in-built advantages, such as no possibility of a zealous husband telephoning one in the night!

Didn't I tell you that Dino was a character? *'Bella, bella,'* I think he was saying, and judging by the gleam in his eye and the flash of all those gold teeth, he didn't mean the little Fiat. Don't worry about all those old wrecks with grass growing up through them. They're just part of the scenery.

April 15

Have now had a chance to examine the sleeper ploy in more detail – indeed I've thought of nothing else! As I feared, the double compartments are only in the Second Class. I should like to have treated you to the best but as you say, Geoffrey might well have been curious had he noticed you were travelling First.

I will make the booking. Mrs Cernik usually looks after such matters. I'll have to pretend I forgot to ask her or something, and reclaim the outlay afterwards. I'm sure that's no problem.

And I'll use your married name. If anything should go wrong, and I can't see how it possibly can, 'Davies' is a much commoner name than 'Godley'. I mean 'Mr and Mrs Davies' wouldn't stand out so strongly in a casualty list or similar! See how I think of everything!

Seriously, it really does seem foolproof. We need not meet until the train departs. I will arrive early and keep out of sight. Then if Geoffrey brings you to the station, as he will insist on doing, you say, it won't matter how long he lingers. I admire that gentlemanly punctilio of his. For all the talk of equality of the sexes, etcetera, I am sure that all *feminine* women like to feel protected and fussed over.

At last the guard will blow his whistle and wave his green flag, if that is still the practice, the train will glide out of the station and you will find your way to our compartment. I shall be waiting for you with a half-bottle of champagne in a plastic bag with some ice cubes – better still, an imperial pint if I can find one; a handy size for two people which the Army & Navy Stores used to stock. Or would something more warming be more appropriate? Anyway, some pleasant surprise – ah, that's a funny thing to say! How can I tell you of my dreams, almost as if you were sitting next to me, it sometimes seems, and yet plan a surprise for you? Truly I begin to live in two worlds!

Our night-cap finished, it will be time to 'turn in'. If you wish, I will stroll along the corridor while you slip into your night apparel, though I hope that in these free and easy times you won't think too much modesty *de rigueur*. We shan't need to toss for the choice of bunks. You shall have whichever you prefer, the top one I expect. I will steady the little ladder for you. And then – well, I would be a hypocrite if I pretended I had no dreams about that, too. I'm only human. But only if you are of a like mind. We are both grown-up people who are aware of our own frailties and our own loyalties. We shall know what is right for the moment. Please believe me when I say what I look forward to more than anything is the intimacy! Oh dear! That sounds worse than ever. I mean 'intimacy' in the nice sense, not as it used to be employed in the *News of the World*.

I mean the things we can talk about as the train rushes through the night. Enclosed in our private world we shall be able to confide and reminisce and laugh together and blurt out all manner of secrets. I shall be able to reach up, and you down, so that our hands clasp. It will be the acme of friendliness I have always longed for, ever since I was a boy. We shall sleep and wake and sleep again. One time the train will be halted in a station, perhaps, the lights bright round the edge of the window blind, the rumble of trolleys on the platform.

In the morning we shall peep out and see the crags and heather of Scotland, and taste the clean cold air. The attendant will bring tea and biscuits. The business of getting up and washing and re-packing one's case, usually so bleak, will be magical and precious. And still breakfast at the station hotel to enjoy together!

Is not the little car running sweetly? Any time you want it done again let me know. The only thing is that Dino seems to have assumed that it was Kate's and made the bill to me. Well, let it be a little going-away present.

April 18

All the omens for the Scottish trip are good! From being initially rather quizzical about my decision to pay a visit to the Toy Fair Walter is now enthusiasm itself. He has put a paragraph in *Toys & Games* to say I'll be there, and we've decided with Foybells, who are marketing it, to give the Scots a sneak preview of *Strip Jill Off!* which wasn't due to be exhibited until the Grosvenor House Show. This is not one of our more intellectual games, I'm afraid! In fact it's only a re-hash of the old card game of Strip Jack Naked, with some rather saucy cards designed by Gilvray Ryman, who used to draw those magazine covers if you remember. To tell the truth I'm not convinced it's what we ought to be doing but Walter say it's only a bit of fun, and quite innocuous. Apparently the idea came to him when his children were playing cards with their own friends the Christmas before last. I just wonder *what* card game they were playing with their friends, that's all.

I'll slip a pack into my brief case and if time hangs heavily on the journey we can always have a hand!

Moreover, it so happens that we're negotiating just now for the printing of our very first books. I don't remember if I went into detail about these with you, I try not to bore friends with too much 'shop'; but briefly it's a series called *It's Fun Being a Field Mouse, It's Fun Being a Woodpecker*, etcetera. They're aimed at first readers, with big print and simple words though the text isn't in the least babyish nor the art work sentimental. In fact the illustrations wouldn't disgrace a scientific wildlife book, except for a slight emphasis, perhaps, on the fluffy young of the various species. They're done for us by a chap in Oxfordshire, called Summerbee, who's an architect, and in my opinion a better painter than an architect! Anyway, to do them justice they've got to be processed and printed very nicely, though of course economically. Walter was all for going to Holland or Czechoslovakia, being a Czech himself originally, then along came this very interesting approach from – yes, you guessed it! Glasgow. An old firm which had always concentrated on letterpress but seeking now to branch out in litho, and very competitive. Walter wants me to go along and get an idea of the equipment they've got and the real calibre of the people who'll do the work, and never mind the smooth young reps they hire to descend on one in London.

So fate is smiling, at last. In forty-eight hours from now – to be exact, fifty – I shall be on my way to Euston. My heart thumps just to think of it!

Chapter Four

April 21

This is the first time I have tried to record these thoughts other than in the Three-Litre humming along the motorway. In the stillness of my hotel room I feel self-conscious. In the next room someone is shaving – I can hear the whirr of the shaver quite clearly. He will be able to hear my voice. I suppose I could be dictating orders, memoranda, etcetera, except that so far I have not been able to bring myself to put in an appearance at the footling little exhibition.

Anyway, what does it matter what anyone overhears? Not any more.

I slipped the recorder into my document case at the last moment. It suddenly struck me that my heart might be so full that I would need to be able to pour out my thoughts at the first opportunity.

Well, here they are, if not quite as intended.

I can hardly bear to think back to the moment when I kissed Kate and the girls goodbye. Little Sam was in bed and asleep, of course, as Miranda should have been. We had enjoyed a supper of sandwiches and coffee in front of the television set, an indulgence we only allow on Sunday evenings. A cheerful fire burned in the grate. The old film was – but I dare say you and Geoffrey will also have watched it. I can't conceal that I felt a pang of regret as I exchanged this cosy domestic scene for the dark night. Once on the road, however, I felt my spirits rise and a lively anticipation grip me. I was in plenty of time and threaded my way through back lanes to get on to the A40 instead of the motorway. It's slower but once one reaches the outskirts of London the access to Euston is much simpler. And it may sound silly but the thought had flashed through my mind that if I passed through Prickwell there was the million-to-one risk of happening to encounter you and Geoffrey also en route!

I left my car in the new underground car park, which is a useful wrinkle if you don't know about it. Providing one gets one's ticket endorsed, the rail traveller gets a substantial discount. I was in such good time that the train was not yet at the platform. As soon as it came in I went aboard meaning to hide myself forward in one of the ordinary compartments for the luckless souls who can't afford sleeper accommodation. To my surprise I found a 'Nightcap Bar' which although it was not yet open for business seemed both a more cheerful and more natural waiting place. In due course some fellow travellers put in an appearance and after some good-humoured prompting the attendant was persuaded to open up and start serving drinks. I had our libation all ready in my bag but felt the occasion called for a little something and asked for a whisky and soda.

There seemed to be a number of regular users of the service who knew each other. In such a convivial atmosphere time ceased to hang so heavily and it was with quite a start that I looked at my watch and saw that there was only fifteen minutes to go. I was filled with a sudden anxiety lest you had not arrived and finishing my drink made my way down the train. The corridor of every coach seemed blocked by stupid people asking each other which were their compartments, or pestering the attendant – they had only to consult the lists displayed at each entrance. I felt my anxiety increasing, but to transfer to the open platform would have been to make myself too obvious.

I arrived at last at 'C' coach and forced myself to go more warily. Just as well I did. Imagine my dismay when I suddenly heard Geoffrey's voice raised not five yards away and next moment saw him emerging from a compartment calling quite clearly, 'I say there!'

Without pausing to think I barged through the nearest door. Inside was an elderly lady with a younger companion, unpacking their things but fortunately not yet *en deshabille*. I blurted out some sort of apology and withdrew at once, quite sure that Geoffrey had already spotted me and cursing myself for behaving in such an obviously guilty fashion. However he was heading the other way down the corridor and you were just following him out of the compartment. I'm sorry if I gaped at you rather foolishly but I was thoroughly disconcerted by now. You must agree that I then acted promptly on your frowned warning and hastily retreated the way I had come.

What an impossible situation! I could only wander miserably up and down 'D' and 'E' coaches, reluctant to withdraw farther but not daring to venture back into 'C'. I was convinced that Geoffrey had 'rumbled' the whole scheme and taken you home. The journey through the night to which I had been counting the hours would now be in solitude, the empty bunk above taunting me all the way to Glasgow. Moreover the attendants in 'D' and 'E' were beginning to eye me suspiciously and ask what berth I sought. I was tempted to quit the train myself, concoct some excuse and drive back to Kate.

But by now it was apparent that the train was about to leave. I risked leaning out of the window and saw Geoffrey walking away – alone! He turned and waved. My heart leaped. As soon as we began to move I hastened along to 'C' again and – well, you know the rest. I tapped on the door of berths 15 and 16 and your voice came instantly, 'Just a minute!' My heart was beating fast. Then out you came, so beautiful but rolling your eyes and putting a finger over your lips to command silence and saying over your shoulder, 'won't be long' – oh, to someone *else*! – and hurrying me back along the corridor to explain.

I take all the blame, though I must say no one could have anticipated Geoffrey's insistence on buying a platform ticket, escorting you right to your coach and then perusing the typewritten list of names and berths. Gentlemanly punctilio can be carried too far in my opinion. No wonder he exploded when he read 'Mr Davies and Mrs Davies'! One can only be grateful that his wrath was directed solely at British Rail and he suspected nothing more deliberate. Of course it helped that the attendant should also have assumed it was a blunder in the booking office. Thank goodness I hadn't previously made myself known to him.

Anyway, I was relieved to learn that the lady he put in with you instead was someone of roughly your own age, and not a fearful old dragon such as I had intruded on. I came face to face with her again when I was trying to resolve my own accommodation problems. She emerged from the toilet and gave the most ridiculous exclamation of dismay, as if I were a sex maniac or something. The attendant was quite unsympathetic enough already.

'Mr Davies, eh?' he said. 'Ah, that was to have been in sixteen?'

'Yes, apparently there was some ridiculous—'

'You can't have that berth now.'

'I wouldn't dream of occup—'

'The lady's husband turned up, y'see. Wasn't half laying about him.'

'I know. I *know*. I have seen Mrs Davies and I wouldn't dream of—'

'There's a Miss Stringer in it now, who was somehow left off the list altogether, lucky we was able to help her.'

'Indeed! How fortunate. The only thing is – what about me?'

'Ah, yes. What name was it again?'

'God –,' I started to expostulate, luckily being able to stop short on the first syllable. In point of fact I rarely blaspheme or use bad language, least of all in front of working people.

'No need to get excited,' the fellow said.

'Davies,' I amended.

'There's no other Davies on the list.'

'Of course there isn't. There was a mix-up.'

He pored over his papers for at least three minutes occasionally muttering and shaking his head. I'm sure it was simply to pile on the agony. Finally he folded them and said, 'You could try my colleague in coach "M". Tell him Fred sent you.'

I had put a half-crown ready in my pocket but I wasn't going to reward that kind of off-hand treatment. To cut a long story short the attendant in 'M' found me an unoccupied berth but so grudgingly that again I resisted the impulse to tip him. Half of it is guilt, you know, and in this egalitarian age there's really no occasion for it. However, I did leave a shilling on the morning tea tray.

My companion of the night was – well, perhaps you noticed me carrying his suitcase along the platform this morning, there being the usual dearth of porters. It was the least I could do, though I must admit I was chiefly anxious not to miss you. He was the gaunt man in the kilt who was following me with the aid of a stick. His name was McMurtie and once I became attuned to his rather heavy brogue I found him excellent company. He is with the Scottish Hydro-Electric Board and told me a number of most interesting things. Did you know that one Highland river – he did give me its name but I have forgotten it – produces as much power as the East Lancashire coalfield? Or it may have been East *Lanarkshire*. Anyway, he is a Fellow of the Institute of Water Engineers and a great angler. He described the catching of one particular salmon in great detail. I had no idea it was such an elaborate pursuit. Just now his style is rather cramped by a very painful 'slipped disc' in his back. As a matter of fact he sought my assistance in loosening a steel corset he has to wear, and in donning it again this morning.

Not quite the kind of intimacy I had hoped for! But before I pressed the 'record' button I resolved that no maudlin self-pity should find a place on the spool, however flat and disappointed I might feel. As I certainly was feeling!

On reflection I agree that you were wise to rule against breakfast together after all. It would hardly have been a very light-hearted repast and, as you said, Jessie was expecting you. But as I registered at the Central Hotel my heart was heavy. Of course it was much too early to have access to my room and I was obliged to wash and brush up in the Gentlemen's cloakroom. I don't mind telling you I had to force myself to whistle a few bars of Dvorak's 'Humoresque' as I shaved. I felt that at all costs I must not give away to despair, or all would be lost.

April 22

How right I was! How ashamed I would have felt when later you telephoned to suggest afternoon tea, a kind and imaginative thought I will never forget. I almost jumped with joy when the hall porter handed me the message, and winged feet bore me to McVittie's tea-rooms! Already we could laugh at the misfortunes of the journey – or at least we could until Jessie finished her shopping and joined us.

Even then you kept on making those humorous references to poor Mr McMurtie and his steel corset. Jessie must have wondered why it should have amused us so. She is the person I remembered from St A and very nice, though, as you hinted before she arrived, a little provincial by our standards. It was kind of her to ask me out to Helensburgh but of course I was committed to the Trade Dinner at the hotel and returning home today. I did not waste a single moment on vain regrets. I am sure the only worthwhile attitude is to be positive and forward-looking. There is always tomorrow.

In the general hilarity I did not tell you much about my visit to Mackay Eldritch, the printers, which was most successful and indeed contributed largely to the much improved spirits I was able to bring to our reunion. Work was proceeding on our first two titles, *It's Fun Being a Field Mouse* and *It's Fun Being a Barn Owl* and I was able to inspect some of the large sheets which will eventually be folded and cut and bound into books. It is not easy to visualize the finished article from such raw material, especially when only one or two of the colours have been printed and the red, say, has still to be added. But I could tell that there was nothing skimped or hasty about what was going on. Afterwards the manager prevailed upon me to have a 'dram' in his office and then repair across the road for lunch.

So, with one thing and another it was late afternoon before I put in an appearance at the Toy Fair. As I had perhaps been unconsciously fearing, *Strip Jill Off!* had not gone down well with every visitor to the Foybells stand. One forgets how the Church – or Kirk, one should say – is so much more involved in everyday affairs in Scotland. I was told many times of disapproving remarks made by the reverend councillor who opened the Fair on behalf of the Lord Provost and subsequently toured the stands. Then in his speech at the Dinner the president of the Scottish retailers added words of reproof which I could hear for myself.

I must say Foybells had chosen to promote the product in singularly tasteless fashion as 'An Old Favourite in New (un)Dress!' I said as much to young Billy Bell, who shrugged the complaint aside. 'We'll hang oor heids,' he said in what was supposed to be a Scottish accent, 'a' the way to the bank' – apparently there had already been quite a number of inquiries. Gratifying as this may be, I personally regret our association with anything dubious just as we are branching out as responsible children's publishers. When a reporter from the *Daily Record* approached me after the dinner I readily gave him a 'quote', as he termed it. I don't know if you will have seen that paper. I brought a couple of copies home with me. The report is on page six, under the heading *Kiddies' 'Strip' Game Rumpus*. They spelled my name wrong, of course, but the gist of it is reasonably accurate. It reads:

> Mr Graham Goddy, who developed the game, said: 'It was not intended for wee children. We hoped it would be exported to countries like Denmark and Saudi Arabia. My partner and I are both family men and churchgoers.'

I trust that Walter will approve, when I show him, but frankly we do not always see eye to eye in matters of taste. His reactions to my *Action Padre* notion have been flippant to put it mildly.

The evening ended with the English contingent, as is so often the case, going 'on the town'. They asked me to join them but I hadn't slept well the previous night; his back injury caused Mr McMurtie to groan out aloud every time the train jolted him, which I found rather disturbing. I preferred to go to bed early and think warmly of a certain party until I fell into a refreshing sleep. Besides, I did not think that many fleshpots would be forthcoming in a city whose elders rightly disapproved of *Strip Jill Off!*

From the bleary eyes and badinage at breakfast this morning it seems that I was wrong, and that some of the chaps ended up in what was to all intents a bordello. They are welcome to their shabby adventures. As I drive home once more along the motorway I count my blessings. Dear Kate always has an extra-delicious supper prepared if I have been away. The children will be agog for the little surprises I always bring back, namely samples from the Toy Fair, postcards of the hotel and a tin of Scotch shortbread. I feel only pity for those unfortunates who feel the need to 'break out' whenever they are away from home. What can compare with the contentment of a pleasant home, a loving wife and children, and a clear conscience?

Chapter Five

Four weeks exactly since I last confided to this little go-
between that never goes between, and therefore four
weeks and a day since last I was in your presence in a
Glasgow tea-shop.

It is not wholly by design. It was not even to be expected.

I mean, we live in the same small town or sprawling
village, whichever you prefer. Shopping in the High Street
of a Saturday morning one meets practically everyone one
knows in Prickwell. The last three Saturdays I have been in
a continuous tingle of expectation and apprehension just as
it used to be in St Andrews all those years ago when one
moped from coffee shop to coffee shop or trailed down to
the pier on Sunday morning in the hope (or dread) of
seeing Rita Whichello or Ann Frayn or (most of all!) Binnie
Lines. But ne'er a glimpse of you.

The same with our old friend British Rail. Two Thurs-
days running I discovered a pressing reason to take the
train into town, the 9.07 of course. Last week I had the
bright idea, instead, of simply driving round the station
car park to see if a little Caravaggio blue Fiat were there. It
wasn't.

Yet all the time I have only to lift the telephone and dial. No doubt I shall.

It is simply that . . . well, our relationship did come to a natural break, as they say on television. One awaits . . . some sort of sign.

Striving to get back into the swing of dictating these thoughts I replayed the last few moments of the last passage, when I was driving home after the Glasgow trip. One was consoling oneself with the reflection that a clear conscience certainly added to the pleasures of homecoming, and so it proved. As the children clung to one in welcome, warm and sweet-smelling from the bath, and Kate was framed smiling in the kitchen doorway, one felt a pang of – well, not relief exactly, nor yet remorse, but of realization that one had perhaps let matters get out of perspective.

Besides, there is one's position in the community – yours as well as mine. It takes little to set tongues a-wagging in Prickwell, though Heaven knows there is no shortage of ammunition. A breath of scandal would be doubly unfortunate just when Kate and I are resolved to take our worship to Pinkney Dene. Imagine the constructions that would be placed on our sudden departure from the Revd. Lumsden's flock. Nor would it help the business as Walter and I prepare to launch our first *It's Fun* titles.

Walter, by the way, was not altogether appreciative of my efforts to atone for upsetting the Scots with *Strip Jill Off!* Apparently young Billy Bell had already telephoned accusing me of disloyalty. It was they who were disloyal, I said sharply, with their cheap promotion 'gimmicks'.

May 27

Five weeks. Last night we were planning our first barbecue of the season. When I mentioned your names Kate said, 'Why?' and added pointedly that we had heard nothing from you since our dinner party. I replied truthfully that I had seen no sign of either of you for weeks, and that perhaps you were away.

Of course, I wouldn't be so ill-mannered as to include that remark of Kate's if there were any chance of your hearing these lucubrations. But the possibility is now even more remote. In any case, as I took care to point out to Kate, you had first asked us to a party; in a sense our dinner was only returning an invitation.

You are not away are you?

May 29

I must say the weather undoes one's sternest resolves. As I get home to the Heath from the stuffiness of London and the fumes of the Autostrada, the scent of the grass and trees and ferns is quite intoxicating. Have I told you about going 'sailing' with Max? Out on the lake, with the sun dappling the water and the breeze ruffling one's hair one feels, even more strongly, the romantic stirrings of one's youth.

May 30

All right, I have tried to ring you, simply to know how you both are, that is all. Three mornings running there was no reply. This morning I tried from home, while Kate was taking Little Sam to school. Without even waiting to find out what I wanted, you said breathlessly, 'I'm sorry, I have to fly. Can you ring later?' – and slammed the phone down.

Very well, my lady, if that's how you want it I shan't trouble you again.

Max Kennerly, of all people, has cleared up one mystery, anyway. He dropped in last night to fix a sailing date this evening and said, quite out of the blue, 'By the way, I didn't know that Mrs Davies we met here worked in Broadbents.'

'Broadbents?' I echoed uncomprehendingly.

'In Windsor. The opticians. Went in to order a new pair of half-frames and for the moment couldn't think who it was grinning at me so cordially.'

'Davies?' said Kate. 'Oh, *those* Davieses. They never returned our invitation. Is she behind the counter, you mean?'

'Not exactly,' said Max. 'More a sort of receptionist to the opthalmist johnny. They're rather grand, are Broadbents. In Wigmore Street as well, you know. What's her name – Binnie, is it? – asked after you both warmly. She's certainly a vivacious lady, even if we did cross swords over your dinner table.'

What's going on? Max is the most strait-laced of chaps and devoted to Sue. But there is no denying he cultivates a considerable charm along with his non-military pose, and I suspect he is more than a little vain. These half-frame spectacles for instance, and tinted lenses into the bargain – well, you'll be able to give chapter and verse but my guess is that they're very special. One would think an army officer might be content with the service issue, which no doubt he would get free.

Now I think about it, there was a great deal of crossing swords for crossing swords' sake on his part, or 'showing off' as I prefer to put it, in that argument he mentioned. What was it about? The end of Empire, etcetera. He was directing most of his sallies at you, I seem to remember, and certainly all the more good-humoured ones.

I've noticed before he has a knack of being able to be gently mocking and yet at the same time give the impression he is flattering one.

Well, he needn't think he is going to sweep you off your feet without a counter-attack, as no doubt he would term it, from this quarter.

On the spur of the moment came off the motorway at
Slough Central and took the new relief road to Windsor. It's
very quick, I dare say you use it every day – or *do* you?
Because, Mrs Davies, there was no sign of you anywhere in
Broadbents. I looked first in the optical department, then
among the cameras, the invalid aids, the dispensary and
the hi-fi and records. I had no idea it was such an
emporium.

What *is* going on?

And to think I have to be affable to him out on the water
this evening. Push him in, more like.

June 4

What a lot of ghosts one little phone call can lay! I simply
asked Mrs Cernik to get Broadbents, the opticians, in
Windsor.

'You mean Broadbents in Vigmore Street?' she
demanded. Mrs Cernik always knows best.

'No, in Vindsor,' I snapped. I was rather pleased with
that, but I thought I'd better soften the barb by saying I
wanted to make an appointment for Kate. After all, Wigmore Street would be much more convenient for me, being
only a short step from our office. In her customary interfer-
ing way she must have asked for the appropriate department before putting me through, because I straightaway
heard your cool accents on the line. Let's hope Mrs C.
didn't stay to listen. What if she did?

So it is mornings only, as your boss does consultations in
Ascot and Guildford and places in the afternoons. He must
be very high-powered. As you say, it is an ideal arrangem-
ent, at least until Geoffrey's abilities are properly recognized at S. C. Rimmer's and duly rewarded. Sometimes I

66

feel we'd be on a much sounder footing if Kate were to contribute a little something to the exchequer. If we had school fees to find, as you do, there'd be no choice in the matter.

And that morning you snapped my head off, you were already late for work, there had already been two phone calls as you were trying to leave and you assumed I was the chap who had been endeavouring to sell Geoffrey an insurance policy.

Anyway, I'll certainly drop in and have a drink with you both on my way home one evening soon. A very pleasant suggestion.

To think I was suspicious of Max! Now this is a confession I really would hesitate to make if I thought you would hear it! I feel quite ashamed of myself, I was so tense and out of sorts last night that I'm afraid I cost him the little race we were competing in. Admittedly, sailing does rather bring out the latent officer in him; he barks very curt instructions to luff and belay and all the other mysterious antics one has to perform! In the clubhouse afterwards, of course, he was as affable as ever. Did I explain about this sailing business? It's only a little Enterprise-class effort Max bought for his boys, he says. One is led to believe he handled rather more exotic craft on various foreign tours. We sail it on the flooded gravel pits over at Walford, if you know them. Doesn't sound very thrilling, I know, and between you and me the clubhouse is little more than a wooden hut with a bar at one end. But actually there is quite an acreage of water there, and one or two well-known figures in the small-boat world are members. It may be that I shall take up the sport on my own account: since one may involve one's wife and children as one's crew it is more 'family' than golf, for instance. Meanwhile I can test my enthusiasm at no cost by crewing for Max, at least until the boys break up from Oundle.

By the way, the water is very deep – one always wears a life-jacket – but remarkably clear and clean, as we discovered on our first outing when I did something hopelessly wrong and we capsized. Max was very sporting about it! At the weekends one often sees wives and families bathing from a little beach not far from the clubhouse. As the vicinity is remarkably unspoiled and deserted, considering its proximity to civilization, it struck me that it might be a good place for a picnic some time. And not too far from Windsor!

June 9

Sorry I haven't yet taken you up on the invitation to drop in at the Beechway for a homeward drink. I was going to tonight then, well, it sounds absurd, but Kate happened to ring me at the office and Mrs Cernik just *had* to ask her, of course, if the eye appointment at Broadbents was satisfactory. Sometimes I think she does it on purpose, trying to stir up trouble.

'What's all this about my eyes?' Kate said in her immediate fashion.

As you can imagine, I was completely nonplussed. I said, 'What do you mean?' just as the penny started to drop. Even alone in my office I felt myself go a fiery red.

'Broadbents.'

'Broadbents?'

'The opticians.'

'Oh yes. In Wigmore Street.'

'No. In Windsor.'

'I'm not sure what you mean—'

'Aren't you? Well, we'll talk about that when you come home!'

'What did you want?' I said.

'It doesn't matter now.' And *clunk*.

Naturally that's left me in a bit of a state. I could kick myself! If only I had taken the trouble to look up the number, ask Mrs Cernik for an outside line and dial it myself. Or said it was for anyone but Kate . . . It could have been a friend . . . Max himself, perhaps. Why not? Mrs Cernik knew of him from various little remarks I had dropped to her or to Walter in her presence. And there would be no 'checking up' dangers there.

I suppose I should rehearse some explanations, which was one of my original motives in setting this little gadget to work. Mrs Cernik could have got it all wrong. It was on Max's behalf I was ringing. Here we go. Now if you would only listen for a moment, my dear, Max asked me to give Broadbents a ring. The famous new specs have got a loose hinge already!

No, that won't do. What's to stop him ringing them himself? Better if it was something that had to be collected, and he couldn't manage it; has had to fly to NATO for a conference or something, as is often the case. I just rang them to make sure the article was ready and save a wasted detour.

The trouble is that Max is always popping in, or Kate might innocently say something to Sue Kennerly. It will have to be someone more remote. Dino the ace mechanic, perhaps? A sliver of metal in his eye? But Kate takes her little car to him herself these days. She'd be sure to ask after his injury next time she saw him . . . Oh, dear, what a tangled web we weave when first we set out to deceive.

June 10

In the event Kate seemed to have quite forgotten the matter. Supper passed very pleasantly with the children. It was only when they had scampered away to watch television that with hardly any change of voice she said quietly, 'Now tell me about Broadbents.'

I took the offensive. 'Mrs Cernik got it all wrong and in future I would be grateful if you would refrain from creating scenes on the telephone in the middle of—'

'You were ringing that Binnie Lines.'

'Of course I was.'

She had gone rather pale. 'At least you might have the grace not to use my name in your wretched deceits—'

I banged my hand angrily on the table, making the crocks rattle. 'If I wanted to see her – which I don't and haven't, as you well know, since our dinner party – what's to have stopped me from ringing their house? As you equally well know, I had no idea until Max told us the other evening that she was working even, let alone where.'

'Exactly. You could never find her in at home.'

'As a matter of fact she only works mornings.'

'How do you know?'

'She happened to tell me!'

'I'm sure she did.'

'Look—'

'Will you please not shout? The children will hear.'

I left the table coldly. Nothing more was said until we were going to bed. Kate – I can see her still – was at her dressing table, which if you remember is a cut-down Victorian shaving table on which she stands a little swing mirror; she dislikes the conventional dressing-table whose large mirror blocks off half the light from the window. I could see her eyes watching me in the reflection.

She said, 'You'd tell me if anything was going on?'

'*Nothing* is going on.'

'That's all I want to know,' she said with what sounded a little like a sob, which is unusual for Kate; she does not often have recourse to such womanly weapons.

I gave a profound sigh and kissed the top of her head. 'If only you would trust me a little more,' I said. 'Or at least let me explain. There's this girl I told you of who's going to do the Stanley books, Veronica what's her name – Hart. Veronica Hart. Blind as a bat. Huge pebble lenses which she's very conscious of. I asked her if she had thought about contact lenses. She said her eyes needed too much correction and weren't they very expensive? So I said I'd try and find out for her.'

She took my hand and pressed it against her cheek. 'I'm sorry,' she murmured.

Of course I forgave her, at once. But as affectionately as one emerges from such misunderstandings, they leave their little bruises. If I am to be suspected whatever I do, I might as well earn that suspicion! But you will understand why I choose to lie low for a day or two.

The funny thing was that the Veronica Hart explanation came to me quite out of the blue. I hadn't prepared it at all. I shall take good care to bring up the subject of contact lenses. Indeed I begin to persuade myself I may have raised it already!

June 13

In the crawl to the Hogarth roundabout the sun beats down from above and the heat from the jam of cars rises up to meet it. The atmosphere is quite blue – Heaven knows how the boys survive who thread their way in and out of our ranks selling evening papers. The drivers all around me are in their shirt-sleeves, sweating and scowling. But just ahead is an exception to the usual homeward-bound commuter, a young chap on a motor scooter with his girl on the pillion. They came filtering up through the cars but here we're packed so close that they can only move with the procession. The girl has fair hair in bunches – neither of them is wearing a crash helmet, silly children. When she puts her feet to the ground her legs are slender and bare. They have

71

some bits of luggage festooning the scooter. I wonder where they are going?

How pleasant it will be to get home into the country, if not as pleasant as last night! As I anticipated – or feared – the summer suits you disturbingly well. It quite took my breath away when you opened the door, brown limbs against crisp lime cotton and such a welcoming smile! Geoffrey was in good form, too.

'Hello, how's the tiddleywinks trade?' he joked. Oh, one gets used to such pleasantries. When the Mugwumps were at the height of their fashion one had to put up with endless repetitions of the catch-phrases. Did you know they were in the Royal Variety performance in 1965, I think it was? In fact most of our labours these days are devoted to rather more intellectual pastimes, if I may say so, plus our publishing venture. But I never mind being teased about the more childish end of the business. The day a toyman feels anything but pride and a sense of privilege in being entrusted with the first entertainment of innocent, eager little minds, I always say, is the day he should look for some other occupation.

Anyway, when I thought to amuse Geoffrey with an account of the ridiculous *Strip Jill Off!* episode in Glasgow I was slightly surprised to discover that he knew all about it. I hadn't appreciated that you would have told him about our meeting there, though of course there was absolutely no reason why you shouldn't. It was silly of me to shoot you that rather startled glance. Luckily, Geoffrey seemed not to notice. The only thing is that I forgot to tell Kate, and it would probably be tactless to repair the omission at this stage. We shall have to make sure the subject doesn't crop up next time we all four get together.

I was also somewhat surprised to gather you've taken to going for a dip in the Fox-Rogers's pool. One can see the temptation, especially when the weather is as gorgeous as it is now, and the nearest decent public baths being at Maidenhead or Slough. But it is only a little tank built up above the ground. Two strokes and you're hitting the other side! Also, as I've hinted before, Mollie and Roderick are not the most upright among Prickwell citizens. One could hear splashings and raucous laughter when we took our drinks on to your patio, which I must say you've made look very elegant with that white iron furniture and comfy lounger.

If there had been a chance I would have proposed our little picnic by the gravel pits, where you could swim in rather more natural surroundings.

Did I gather that Geoffrey had been playing golf that evening I would have called had it not been for that absurd scene that Kate made? I wasn't listening carefully. It was only afterwards I began trying to work it out. You had that little tiff, if you remember, about the ice-cube tray not having been re-filled.

It is too galling.

At last we're on our way. The girl on the back of the scooter has her head tucked against the back of her companion's neck as I overtake them. I am filled with a sort of nervous impatience. I must hurry or it will be too late. But for what? I am not sure.

It occurs to me that if one drives round by the Beechway and providing the garage hasn't yet been cleared out, one would be able to see who is at home from the cars parked in the drive: your little Fiat, Geoffrey's white Triumph 2000, isn't it?

Later

Both there.

Just as I was planning things to allow me a nice early departure this evening, of course Walter had to ask me to stay and help entertain Zillah Graves and her tiresome husband. Why they have to be entertained at all I don't see. If Walter wants to take them out to dinner, as he is even now, along with his wife (i.e. Walter's wife whose name is Wendy, very English) I suppose that is his lookout as long as he doesn't cane the partnership for the whole lot. I am always most scrupulous about expenses, only put in one of those lunches we had together, for instance, the one at Casa Nostra with all the garlic. Well, the accountant likes proper bills, it's a pity to waste them.

What was I saying? Oh yes, accepting the dinner if we must, and actually everybody else has been making a fuss of old Zillah, like her literary agent and her publishers and the BBC because believe it or not the Mugwumps are ten years old this week, I don't see why there had to be the red carpet unrolled and the drinks cupboard unlocked in Walter's office as well. Half past five they came, on the dot, and they were still there when I finally and eventually presumed to leave, and now it is seven, um, nineteen and though there shouldn't be any hold-ups, at this time of day, even if I get a clear road it'll be damned near eight before I hit Prickwell and if old Geoffrey has been having a few holes up at the golf course he'll no doubt be toddling home again just about then.

I've never been one for office tippling and nor, to do him justice, has Walter. That little hospitality cupboard of ours will stay unopened, oh, for weeks on end. Once you start needing a little something to blunt the edges of the day you're on the downward slippery slope, no doubt about that, no doubt about that at all. Mrs Comrade Cernik, of course, is in her element on these occasions, her eyes gleam

74

like humbugs, Parkinson's Old-Fashioned Mint Humbugs if you are familiar with such delicacies. Furthermore she pins a bloom to her corsage, an enormous tropical *puce* bloom no doubt obtained from Kew Gardens where she lives, in Kew. We let her officiate at these little occasions as she enjoys them so and in theory it helps to put visitors' ladies at their ease, though if I know Zillah Graves she'd be happiest with a gathering of giant all-in wrestlers. She was pawing this new husband of hers – there's no other word for it – in the most sickening fashion. He's an Australian, of course, as one might guess. Not that it any way affects the sentimental rubbish she talks about her wretched Mug-wumps.

'Do you know,' she hooted, 'what dear Andrew Joyner told us? He said there was nothing he was prouder of, in all his time in broadcasting, than the changes he'd been privileged to help bring about in children's programming, and in particular' – no prizes for guessing what was coming – 'and in particular the pleasure and grounding in good citizenship which The Mugwumps had given to so many millions of kiddies.'

'Not to mention,' I said, 'the fact that today's little innocent faces are tomorrow's clientele.'

Well, that didn't go down too well at all, though in fact it is only a line from a satirical song of Tom Lehrer's that was the rage when we were at St Andrews, wasn't it? 'Never knock the product, son,' said the husband fellow and Zillah chimed in, 'I wish we could be sure whose side Graham is on!'

But if Walter or I happened to mention anything else we were doing, oh that was brushed aside. Of no importance! Do you know what that woman did? The first proof copies of *It's Fun Being a Fieldmouse* and *It's Fun Being a Barn Owl* had just arrived, we'd scarcely had a chance to glance at them, or enjoy what should have been a moment of great satisfaction for us. Walter diffidently showed them to Zillah and without even looking she just swept them into her great leather bag with a 'Charming, charming, I must study them later.' Swept them in, she did.

I only hope Walter will have kept his wits enough to recover them.

Ah, what does it all matter? As a matter of fact a strange fatalism overtook me. I'd been eyeing the clock at first, I don't mind admitting, but Mrs Cernik kept saying, 'Another visky, Mr Godley, or vill it be wodka zis time?' and Walter is always amusing company when he wants to be.

I had this feeling that the evening was out of my hands somehow, I only needed to swirl with the current. I was really quite enjoying the party.

Quite suddenly I knew it was time to leave. I said, 'Goodbye, everyone,' gathered up my bits and pieces and made straight for the lift, not even calling in at our little cloakroom, which was perhaps a mistake. To tell the truth, I really ought to pull up and pop behind a tree but that's not exactly encouraged on the old Autostrada, is it?

Never mind, the Three-Litre responds to my touch like a thoroughbred. I speed to whatever destiny has ordained. Hurry, hurry, hurry!

Later

Oh, God, what now?
I stopped at Heston services for coffee and something to eat, which was just common sense, common sense. Maybe had forty winks in the car park afterwards, also very sensible, drat these office parties. What time is it? Good God, I must have slept longer than I thought. Or perhaps I went to the sailing club for some fresh air, that's it – no, Max might have been there this evening, might even have been asking after me, anyway it's as far as to go home.

What about Walter asking if I would mind joining them for dinner . . . to make up the four. The husband fellow didn't come after all. Or we decided to include Mrs Cernik and thus needed a sixth, that's better. But why didn't I ring Kate and tell her? What if she rang them, after I'd left? Besides the next time she happens to talk to Mrs C. the cat is sure to be out of the bag. I stopped at Heston motorway services, had two black coffees and a hamburger. No, a sandwich.

Oh God, help me to get it right. I feel so sick. I must have a bath.

Chapter Six

How to begin? It would be difficult enough at the best of times, impossible when what should be golden memories are somehow lost and only the moments linger which draw one down to earth again. Fitfully, as in a dream I recall . . .

No, that won't do. If there is any point in this exercise it is surely that one should be absolutely honest with oneself. Let one make it clear that one wasn't drunk or anything like it. One has not been the worse for drink since one's youth, and then only once or twice. One has more respect for the body God gave one. But there is no doubt that Mrs Cernik's measures are unnecessarily large, also that she is assiduous in replenishing one's glass.

My head has been muzzy all day and I have had to drink innumerable glasses of water.

Nor was one in any sense unfit to drive one's car home. If anything I am over-zealous about such matters, and never press 'one for the road' upon departing guests. And as I was explaining to Kate, should ever I have reason to doubt my own hundred per cent alertness I immediately pull up for a breath of fresh air, or, better still, find a cup of strong coffee and a bite to eat. But agreed, one's defences were less well manned than usual, one's restraints somewhat cast to the wind! There was also the embarrassing fact that even if the drinks had not gone unduly to one's head they had certainly gone somewhere! I have noticed this once or twice before and should have learned my lesson and made sure one washed one's hands before setting off. The trouble is that while one is sitting at the wheel one is lulled into a false sense of security. Only as one gets on one's feet, especially in the cool of the evening, is one made aware of extreme urgency. I hope I didn't alarm you jiggling on the step and then rushing straight for the bathroom as you opened the door!

How undignified! But one must see the funny side, as you always do, I will say. And who knows? – perhaps my plight awoke in you some fondness that might never be prompted by one who is always cool and calm.

Such was my preoccupation that I believe I had scarcely noticed whether two cars or only one stood outside your house.

As I came down you said, laughing, 'There is a downstairs loo if only you'd stopped to listen.' Then you offered me a drink and I asked if a cup of coffee were possible and followed you into the kitchen. While you put the kettle on I suppose I blathered something about the office party, then demanded to know where Geoffrey was.

'Playing golf,' you said.

'Back soon?'

You gave me that laughing, open look of yours as if you could read my mind. 'Never know with him. It's a competition but he went straight up there. He probably won't stay for the socializing afterwards.'

'But not just this minute. He won't be finished yet,' I heard myself saying in a sort of thick voice.

'Black or white?' you asked over your shoulder as you spooned Nescafé into a mug.

'Black, it had better be.'

I came up close behind you and put my arms round your waist, taking care to avert my breath in case it smelled too strongly of alcohol. You did not object. You only said 'Don't jog me, it's boiling.'

I kissed the back of your neck. The skin was warm and fragrant. I could feel your delicious firm sit-upon against my thigh – but I must not continue in this vein or I will find myself heading for the Beechway a second night running!

'Sugar?' you asked.

'What?'

'Sugar?'

'Oh, no thanks.' I've always assumed the bitterer the better, so to speak.

You turned and faced me with that steady, amused gaze again. You said, 'Won't Kate be wondering where you are?'

'She knows I had to stay for the party.'

'I just wouldn't feel very relaxed doing anything at the moment.'

If I looked startled – for you laughed again – it was not that I haven't knocked about the world as much as any man of my age, simply that – well, one does not always meet such directness. Also I was feeling suddenly rather strange. The coffee was doubtless sobering but it also made me feel rather sick. I've never been too keen on 'instant' and my heart was bumping with excitement.

'Not in my own home,' you explained theatrically and laughed. 'Besides Geoffrey might be back any sec.'

I must have looked crestfallen for you smiled more warmly now and said, 'He's bound to have some trips away coming up.'

I nodded. There's always a next time, never a this time. Just then the telephone rang. It gave me quite a cold spasm inside, I don't know why. I suppose I thought it might somehow be Kate, anxious and divining where I might be.

80

When I heard you answering conversationally, and feeling rather weak in the knees, I took my coffee back into the lounge and sat down. As soon as I had consumed it I would be off. To put matters bluntly, a lot of explaining to do and nothing to show for it. I closed my eyes and was alarmed to find the room starting to tilt and revolve.

Dimly I heard the *ping* of the phone being replaced. You were standing above me. You said, 'That was Geoffrey. He rang to say he won't be back until nine.'

June 20

What I forgot to record last time was that Kate turned out not to be in the least suspicious, merely rather impatient with my being somewhat out of sorts as a result of Mrs Cernik's measures. She packed me off to bed, where I was not sorry to go. By supper time last night, of course, it had become a family joke, which I am not at all sure was very wise of Kate. A little good-humoured teasing I can enjoy with the best, but one's children should not be taught to disrespect one.

'*I'm* not going to drink alcohol, ever,' said Janet, who can be a little priggish at times.

'*Eeeugh*, it tastes foul,' said Miranda.

'Did Daddy sick?' asked Little Sam.

'No, he did *not*.'

'It's why he brought Mummy those flowers, though,' said Miranda, who can be much too knowing.

Well, this time she doesn't know it all, thank goodness!

This is our secret. Already it is a golden memory. I find myself grudgingly counting the hours that have passed since we tasted that moment of bliss. Forty-six, of which sixteen fled in sleep. At the same time let us not pretend that all was perfect. One was not exactly at one's best . . .

Next time will be better, I promise you. We shall not be

81

furtive, nor rushed nor apprehensive. Instead of cushions spread in a dining annexe, out of the way of neighbours' eyes, we shall lie under the sun and sky by the rippling waters.

June 23

Guess what now! Zillah Graves telephoned Walter as soon as she noticed, she said. I prefer to believe she waited until she felt able to enjoy the moment to the full. I can just hear her cooing, 'By the way I hope you won't mind my mentioning it but I think there's been a *teeny* muddle with your *lovely* picture books . . .' It seems that one of the illustrations to *It's Fun Being a Field Mouse* was accidentally put into *It's Fun Being a Barn Owl* and vice versa, and that the one in *It's Fun Being a Field Mouse* actually shows young field mice being rather messily eaten by a family of owls – as I told you, we set out to make the illustrations realistic as well as appealing.

It is extremely disheartening, and of course some blame attaches to yours truly, as Zillah no doubt took good care to point out, in that I saw the proof sheets in Glasgow and should have spotted the error, though how anyone encountering these mysteries for the first time can be expected to take in every detail straightaway beats me. Each one represents thirty-two, or even sixty-four – I forget which – pages of the finished book, at least half of them upside down from whichever side one happens to be looking, and in some cases not all the colours had been added.

Luckily we were just in time to prevent the binders starting work, but it is obvious that the sheets have got to be printed all over again which is going to add to the cost and will also delay our getting the finished product out to the trade. It *is* disheartening. I badly need cheering up. I think I may drop by.

All today I felt – what is the expression? Ten feet tall! I could not help it. Memories of last evening haunted me so that the infernal Mrs Cernick actually said something to the effect that Mr Godley was such miles avay she vas certain 'e vas in love. I would have snapped, 'But not with you, madam' had not Walter exchanged a sympathetic glance with me behind her back. He had assumed that it was the *It's Fun* mishap that still distracted one. Well, it does remain a worry, of course it does, but last evening helped considerably to put matters in perspective.

How you laughed when I told you of the mix-up! I had to see the funny side myself. And your laughter seemed to speed the light-headedness that your gin-and-tonic had started. Didn't you once say that you had to be squiffy, as you put it, before you could be in the least abandoned? You lacked not squiffiness last night . . .

One must instantly change the subject or one will go off the road.

Actually, Walter is being very sporting about the colour plates business. We are not going to let it get us down. Indeed we are forging ahead with *Stanley the Suburban Squirrel*, which one has mentioned once before and which is to be a story with pictures that one personally believes will be a great success and lead to a whole series of Stanley books.

That Geoffrey should be safely absorbed in a match was something I had dared not hope for. Your legs were so brown and smooth beneath that flimsy, shimmering dress of yellows and greens and white.

Actually, he was Kate's idea originally: Stanley, that is. When we lived in Pipkin Lane and Smailes the demon despoiler was tearing down trees every day to carve out what is now Nuthatch Gardens, the children used to wonder what would happen to the squirrels that one watched scampering up and down the trunks and leaping from branch to branch, etcetera. One expressed the hope that a few might survive in the remaining trees and Miranda, I think it was, elaborated. 'Praps they could live in the telegraph poles,' she said. 'And eat the nuts people put out for the birds,' added Janet. At this point Kate said, 'What a good idea for a children's story', and one must say one saw the possibilities straightaway: the symbolic conflict between nature and encroaching civilization, for instance . . .

After I had caressed you for a while you rested your hand on . . . me and said, 'How are you then?' Just like that. No, with a slight emphasis: 'How are *you* then?' I can hear your voice still; so matter of fact and yet so confidential, the most provocative thing anyone has ever said to me.

So, to cut a long story short, when we thought of venturing into publishing one persuaded Kate to sit down and write one or two chapters. She had always made up such amusing stories and fancies for our children when they were tiny. If the truth were known Little Sam would still enjoy them, however he may pretend to disdain the Chief Sam and all his works! The strange thing was that as soon as she set pen to paper it wasn't quite the same. A tape-recorder yielded scarcely happier results. It wasn't *impossible*. One mustn't seem unappreciative or disloyal. But perhaps the interval between inspiration and execution had been too long. And as Walter put it, this particular subject would be in a sense a children's *satire*, it would need a slightly acid tone that Kate, bless her, could no more feign than she could – oh, have an affair with the milkman!

When I implored you to take everything off you said, 'And suppose Liz Merrill pops in through the french windows? She often does, you know – to borrow a cigarette or have a gossip.' I hadn't thought of that. I felt quite a silly flutter of panic, an impulse to run away. But you were saying, 'You'll have to take me as I am.' I have thought and thought about that ever since. Was the double meaning deliberate? What an unfathomable enchantress you are.

So Walter found this Veronica Hart – the girl with the thick glasses I was going to send to Broadbents, if you remember. She's the daughter of some old friend of his, and apparently very talented though one would never guess it from meeting her. She writes and illustrates, mostly in the teenage magazines and so on. Of course, we shall have to feed her with local colour and amusing things that the children say, etcetera.

Another thing I keep thinking about is your laughing and when I whispered 'Why?' your 'Nothing, nothing,' though I could still feel the ripples of mirth in you. I thought of it only as a moment of beauty.

Afterwards, it's true, I may have been a little subdued and rather anxious to be on my way. But as you yourself pointed out, quite briskly, Kate would be expecting me. There are times when I wish I knew what you really meant.

Actually it was hardly seven-thirty by the time I got home, which was so normal as to occasion no comment. And with the hot weather, nothing more natural than one should head straight for the shower and a change of attire before joining the family for supper. The children were in merry mood; Janet and Miranda had brought back some of their dreadful school jokes and were vying to shock their parents. I suppose one should have been shocked at some of the words they employed, but for all her rather uncompromising views in some respect Kate is curiously broad-minded in others, while I was understandably a little preoccupied.

After they had gone to bed Kate demanded to know what was the matter. Luckily I was able to blurt out the story of the colour plates. She said she knew there was something wrong the moment I came in. Phew!

Ten feet tall again! And this time I could laugh with you, because you had explained what amused you. Ever since Lionel Brechin first led you astray at St Andrews, you said, you had been unable to put out of your mind a mental picture of how absurd one must look, grappling about. I saw the incongruity straightaway, though it would be a pity if one were to be blinded for any length of time to the beauty and solemnity of – dare I say it? – love.

I am sure you are not, deep down.

I blame that bounder Brechin. He would leave anyone with distorted values. Personally I could never imagine what you and all the other bejantines could see in him. I suppose it was the kilt and the hairy legs and the quite unfounded reputation as a poet and scratch golfer.

There is so much I would love to learn about you, and all the things that have happened to you in the twenty years our lives have gone their separate ways. But in your company time races by and all too soon we have to part.

No, that's not strictly true. One might as well be honest if one is going to confide these thoughts at all.

Until we . . . until it happens, I am very tense, I know. I hear a flat, strained voice droning from my head. It is me but it is not me. Do I look strained too? And afterwards – well, it would be pointless to risk lingering needlessly.

I will relax. Next time.

I quite understand about my car, by the way. It had already occurred to me that leaving it too often outside your house might invite comment. On the other hand, if Geoffrey were ever to arrive home unexpectedly, its presence would be both more open and more natural. One could say one had just dropped in to discuss a reunion with other St Andreans in the neighbourhood, for instance. We shall have to play this, as they say, by ear.

After drawing a blank two nights running, at last an unaccompanied Fiat! I forced myself to drive on and park opposite 'Biggles's Stack', that's got the For Sale notice up, about four plots away from you. I was rather proud of this ploy. There must be a regular flow of prospective purchasers drawing up outside. I even made myself pause and pretend to look appraisingly at the property before sauntering casually back, though I must say that of all the despoiler Smailes's standard executive-type designs this one with the reconstituted stone chimney feature is the least desirable. I mean, your house is perfectly individual without any pretension.

But what was this? No one in, despite the evidence of the little Fiat? I began to brace myself for yet another disappointment. Then as I rang again I heard your voice, 'Just a minute,' and through the hammered glass of the door I could see the blur of what looked like bare flesh replaced by the flash of some blue garment.

Whose good resolutions would withstand that?

'Oh, it's you,' you said clutching the housecoat or whatever about you. You had been in the garden catching up on a bit of sun.

'In your nothings?' I queried. I was trying.

Hardly, you laughed, having regard to certain of one's neighbours.

'It is they would be doing the regarding,' I observed, which I think you missed, having started to tell me about working late at Broadbents and their wanting you to do something else I didn't catch, because I am afraid you had let the housecoat part to reveal the briefest of bikinis. End of good resolutions.

And afterwards, as I straightened my tie and combed my hair, that sudden slam of a car door just outside. One's heart turned over. It was only one of the Merrills next door, but I get the message: we shall have to be more careful. As you pertinently asked, how would I feel if it were my drawing-room and Kate quite capable of coming home any moment?

Three times I've driven by; twice the two cars have been in the drive, once his alone. Each time I have had to go the length of the Beechway, to where it ends in a meaningless blob of concrete, and there manoeuvre to drive back. The lock on the Three-Litre is just insufficient and always I need to execute a laborious three-point turn. There are never less than six children on various wheeled toys, whooping and shouting and staring rudely at me.

Also, Max Kennerly keeps asking me to crew for him in the evenings. I cannot go on putting him off.

Friday is Geoffrey's poker night at the club, didn't you say?

Just once more and the demon will be satisfied, I know. We shall be able to laugh and gossip and talk about old times just as we did before.

Meanwhile I think of nothing else. Supposing I talk in my sleep! The possibility terrifies me. When we first married Kate once or twice reported, teasingly, phrases I had muttered in the night. What if I were to blurt your name out or worse? When I woke the other morning I was aware of her thoughtful gaze from the next pillow. I said, 'Is anything the matter?' and there was a pause before she replied that of course there wasn't, she had only been trying to think what we should give Little Sam for his birthday.

It is six-thirty as the fast lane opens up clear of the small bottleneck where the flyover sinks back to earth and a last injection of traffic filters in from Gunnersbury or wherever.

The sun winks blindingly off glass and chrome. My hands slither wetly on the wheel.

All I can say is that it would never have happened if I'd had any inkling she was to be installed so soon. I remember perfectly well your saying that Broadbents wanted you to carry on through the summer and indeed give them a couple of afternoons as well. If, as you maintain, you also pointed out that the children would be coming home for the holidays and you would have to think of something, then I must accept that. I will admit one's mind was on other matters at the time. But I am quite sure you gave me no indication it was all so imminent. I had always understood private schools broke up after the state schools since they go back so very much later. Or so it was in my day.

As for more than a week having elapsed since last we met, that was hardly for want of trying on my part. As I described in detail in my last meditation, could you hear it, five or six times had I reconnoitred the Beechway in vain. Then at last – the little Fiat standing alone. I parked opposite 'Biggles's Stack' again and hurried back. I thought I'd look in the garden first, in case you were sunning yourself again. Also one does feel slightly conspicuous waiting at the front door.

The french door into the lounge stood open. I hesitated only a moment and stepped inside.

Thinking over your question as to what I called out, I am sure it was only something quite innocuous such as 'Hullo, it's me!' or 'Coooeee.' I definitely did not say anything about were you decent, I hoped not. That was the time before.

Venturing upstairs was perhaps a little presumptuous. My reasoning was that if you were enjoying a little rest yourself, or applying make-up, etcetera, you wouldn't thank me for making you jump up and come down. But I did not storm into your or any other bedroom. I simply heard a rustle and catch of breath and popped my head round the appropriate door.

I fully accept that your mother was startled, though I doubt if she need have looked quite so terrified. It wasn't as if she were in any extreme state of undress, nor was I aware that I particularly resemble Jack the Ripper or the Boston Strangler! To tell the truth, I was pretty startled myself. For an instant I thought I must somehow have entered into the wrong house. I remember exactly what I said, which was 'Oh dear, I was looking for Mr or Mrs Davies. Do excuse me.'

I then started to descend the stairs again and your mother emerged wrapping a dressing-gown round her, and mumbling rather hysterically, 'Just a minute, you!'

Of course I still didn't know who she was, but I could at least be sure it was the right house, so I said, 'Geoffrey's not in, then?'

She said something about him being out.

'Binnie, then?'

'She's with him, of course.'

I said, 'Oh dear' again, and then, 'But it's Friday.'

Yes, I know that may have sounded a little odd. I still can't see why your mother should have attached such sinister implications to it. You may also assure her that I did not even notice she had taken her dentures out.

As I had regained the ground floor by now, it seemed logical to be on my way without more ado and let her resume the little rest which, as you say, she needed after the long hot journey from Poole. One planned to introduce oneself formally at some more auspicious date, as I hope may still be the case; she struck me as a charming person. But of course I fully intended to leave word as to who had called, even before she screeched, 'Who shall I say it was? *Who* are you?'

'Graham,' I called up, 'Graham Godley.' I can't think where she got the idea that I said 'Nobody'.

Obviously I'm very sorry if I disturbed her, though one would have thought that in this democratic age she would have become accustomed to neighbours popping in and out of each other's homes. Perhaps a block of flats is rather different. I also see that Geoffrey would have been puzzled as to who the caller might have been. It was a relief to gather that he is always sanguine about such matters and soon shrugged off the mystery with the supposition that it was Roddy Fox-Rogers or someone breezing in to borrow ice-cubes or a lemon. If, as I seemed to detect between the lines of what you were saying, he tends to be a little impatient with your mother, this is to everyone's advantage.

Incidentally, it was perfectly proper of you to ring me at the office; as long as one doesn't make a habit of it. It was obviously necessary to get the matter cleared up. I only wish I could have been as precise then as I have been now, but one can never be sure how much attention Mrs Cernik is lavishing on one.

So you and Geoffrey had popped along to the Jamiesons in Vicarage Gate to see the moonshot, as the Press call it, on colour television. It certainly is a historic occasion, as I tried to impress on the children when I got home and found them watching the same event, albeit in humble black and white. Personally, one is deferring the question of a colour set until all the channels have the facility.

This morning we also watched the expedition on the surface of the Moon. Again, what an awe-inspiring moment! 'It is the start of a new chapter in the history of exploration,' I said. At the same time I could not help reflecting that our own adventures had willy-nilly come to the close of a chapter. Clearly one must lie low for some time before daring to call in the Beechway again. Even my old dream of a picnic by the sailing pits will have to be deferred if the Kennerly boys are going to be out on the water and liable to recognize one. Then there are holidays. Are you going away? We are looking forward to our usual fortnight in St Trevor. One can only . . . send one a postcard.

Chapter Seven

September 8

Just to see you again brought such a confusion of feelings – on top of quite enough confusion already! Granted the necessity of sooner or later having to meet your mother again and make friends, one wouldn't normally have chosen an occasion when one was surrounded by one's own nearest and dearest!

Had we been planning to go to the Harvest Fayre I am sure it would have occurred to me that you might all put in an appearance, and I would have prepared myself accordingly. But Kate having lately transferred the family churchgoing from Prickwell to Pinkney Dene, I assumed she would wish to give the Fayre a miss this year, especially as the Kennerlys were involved in some regatta. Also, when we have visitors from the big city we prefer to take them on the heath after lunch for a breath of real country air.

Actually, it was the presence of a visitor which tipped things the other way – Veronica Hart, the rather plain girl with the thick glasses who was tagging along behind us, in case you didn't register the name in the hurly-burly of introductions, Veronica is doing *Stanley the Suburban Squirrel* for us, in fact she's nearly finished. Kate had nevertheless been holding forth on all the Prickwell types who ought to be incorporated into the saga and suddenly clapped her hands and said, 'But we must take you along to the fête this afternoon, for they'll all be there!'

I said, 'Is that wise, dear?' Old Lumsden can be quite unpleasant and unfortunately he had been very quickly made aware of our defection, if you can call it that, thanks to the officious Wing-Commander Wilshaw who is in charge of the Christian Stewardship arrangements. The moment he noticed our standing order hadn't been paid he was on the phone to ask if the bank had made a mistake! But Kate has never been one to be afraid of anything or anyone, and between you and me she rather enjoys descending on Prickwell events in which she used to be deeply involved and from which she can now feel . . . well, pleasantly at one remove. She sees her old acquaintances running the same old side-shows, etcetera. And of course the children were overjoyed at the prospect of spending money uselessly.

So there we were, one's personal radar only on the look-out for Lumsden. What a good turn-out there was, incidentally. Inner differences of opinion must not blind one to the fact that he has some extremely loyal and hard-working parishioners, as indeed one formerly tried to be oneself. I've never seen The Glebe so thronged.

We were just moving on from the First Aid display, which I must say I thought a little unsuitable – all that emphasis on the 'Kiss of Life'. Some of the comments one overheard! Anyway, Kate was telling Little Sam that if he only picked a dolly's hot-water bottle from the bran-tub that was the luck of the draw, one cannot expect to be favoured every time; also that if he chose to waste his pennies rolling them on the Roll-the-Penny stand it was no good hoping to get a compassionate refund just by crying – when suddenly, who should that be face to face with us on a collision course?

I suppose that for a millionth part of a second I contemplated evasive action, but already I could see the dawning recognition in your mother's eye, not to mention your own characteristic look of amusement. In the same infinitesimal portion of time I took in your children, whom I had never seen before, realized that Kate had spotted you and was painfully aware that Little Sam had started to make a scene. Being the youngest as well as the only boy I sometimes fear that he has been rather spoiled. Actually it probably helped in that Kate was distracted and consequently couldn't register everything your mother said.

'I know *you*,' she loudly proclaimed, and to you, 'That's him!' I must say it was most resourceful of you to ignore her and cry, 'Mummy, you remember Graham Godley, don't you?' as if harking back to far-off student days. '*I* certainly remember *her*,' I broke in heartily. 'The charming Mrs Lines, as I recall. You haven't changed a bit!'

Making to kiss her was, on reflection, over-doing things a little; I had hoped to lodge some discreet plea in her ear. In the event she ducked aside with a stage whisper the whole world must have heard. 'What did I tell you? He's the one!'

I thought my number was up then, but you chipped in quickly. 'You're thinking of Lionel Brechin, Mummy, and anyway that was *ages* ago.' Before she could reply, the Revd. Lumsden chose that instant to broadcast over the public address system, something about bowling for the pig. Talk about divine intervention! Kate made a somewhat icy allusion to the incident later but luckily was only too ready to accept that yes, it was yet another reference to boring St Andrews.

I will say that your mama played up sportingly thereafter. Perhaps you were able to give her a nudge, perhaps it was Kate's genuine flair for putting everyone at their ease on these occasions. She was almost the only lady wearing a long summer dress and I really felt proud to be by her side, so feminine and airy and gracious was she.

Not that you weren't as disturbing as ever in those gay striped slacks – or tights, more like! – and shirt. Once I had recovered from initial trepidation, indeed, I found myself eyeing your bare feet in their sandals, and how you looked from behind, sauntering along, and the way more than one male head turned as you passed, and reminding myself with awe that not so very long ago I had touched and thrilled to those very charms. It was an exhilarating and at the same time tantalizing thought!

Thank goodness the children failed to realize who you were until after we had gone our separate ways. The chorus of whooping and silly jokes was bad enough then. Your children, in contrast, were models of behaviour. Let me get it right: Rebecca is fourteen and at Bramley and Robin is nine and at the prep school in Kent whose name I forget.

As I believe I have said before, my mind is quite made up to send Little Sam away when the time comes. The things they pick up in the village schools! Guess what Miranda came out with the other day? It seems they had been looking up rude words in some dictionary they're given. One particular coarse little word – I am sure you can deduce which one – is apparently defined as 'a small explosion between the legs'.

One had to smile, but as I pointed out to Kate, it is not even very exact. I remember, in my day, the definition at least included the verb 'to emit'.

Veronica Hart seemed to enjoy herself, as far as one can tell with her. She always strikes me as a rather undemonstrative girl, typical of her generation. You know, takes it all for granted, no sense of wonder – and always saying 'you know' just as I've just done. The trouble with sloppy speech is that it is so catching. Kate seems to have taken a great liking to her, I can't think why, and has asked her to come for the weekend next time. Apparently she lives in some squalor in a boat on the Thames. There was one slightly awkward moment when Kate asked how she was getting on with changing to contact lenses – which, if you remember, I was supposed to have arranged with your firm! Luckily she has in fact seen some specialist about being fitted.

I must tell you of one extraordinary coincidence: can you guess what car she arrived in? Yes – yet another Fiat 500, Caravaggio blue!

September 12

Now that at last I've had the chance to make friends with your mother, I must say she's most charming. The flowers were a very sound idea on your part. I remembered a little nursery on the Bath Road that one used to pass before the motorway was completed; whatever the time of day or night they seemed to be open for business, and there were always two or three cars parked outside as homegoers who had no doubt forgotten birthdays or anniversaries hastily repaired the omission. Or perhaps by cutting out the middleman one gets better value. Anyway, your mother seemed pleased with the marigolds, and at nine shillings the large bunch one can't grumble.

She told me she had been working hard to pull your garden into shape while she had been with you, rather implying that Geoffrey might spend a little less time at the golf club. While loudly praising what she had done I took good care to show where one's loyalties lay. 'But Mrs Lines,' I said, 'when one's been working as hard as we all have to work these days, one needs one's relaxation. That in my case it happens to take the form of pottering around the house and garden is simply my good fortune. It could just as easily have been golf or sailing.' I said it was very important that he should make the most of the light evenings while they lasted.

As it certainly is! Incidentally, while your mother was telling me at length about the garden at Lewes she had before your father passed on I couldn't help noticing the invitations and fixtures, etcetera, on the mantelpiece. I made a mental note of several dates on which Geoffrey is due to be playing. Wish one had thought of it before, as it would have saved many fruitless detours.

With Robin and Rebecca back to school by the end of the week, all that remains is for Mama to return to Poole. I must say I am a little disconcerted to find she has no immediate plans. I said how lucky she was to live by the sea and no doubt she would be looking forward to enjoying the last of the fine weather there, but she only muttered something about your being too tired to cook when you came in, and that left to yourselves neither you or Geoffrey would have a proper evening meal.

Personally, I think it is a great mistake for grandparents to be allowed to imagine they are indispensable. When Kate was in and out of hospital in the early years of our family, her mother became very possessive. In the end Kate herself had to put her foot down. It was one of the reasons we were both rather relieved when the plan for a 'granny annexe' in Pipkin Lane fell by the wayside.

How does Geoffrey get on with your mother, I wonder?

I assured her that in our experience you were a very good cook, and in any case there was now a Chinese take-away place in Prickwell High Street which was supposed to be reasonable. At which point you arrived home. If you remember, your mother was insisting there was no substance in Chinese food, half an hour after you'd eaten you were hungry again. I said, 'I'm hungry right now,' with a suspicion of a wink in your direction. I could see by the look in your eyes you got the message!

Making my farewells I said, 'Hope to see you next time you come to Prickwell, Mrs Lines,' and she said, 'I hope so, too,' so perhaps all will be well. If not, one must press ahead with the picnic idea.

September 18

Feeling in need of some cheering up last evening, I waited until Mrs Cernik had left and dialled your number. I thought that if your mother answered I could simply ring off. In fact it was Geoffrey's voice, which rather threw me. I very nearly blurted out, 'Is Mrs Lines there?' but by great fortune got into such a muddle that I said 'Mrs Poole' instead. Association of ideas! Geoffrey said, 'Mrs *Who*?' which gave me the chance to collect my wits and pretend I'd got the wrong number. It occurs to me one might use the ploy in other situations, taking care to disguise one's voice by means of a handkerchief over the mouthpiece. Or one could practise various accents on this little machine. Och aye, and would Mistress McTavish be at home? She is what? Och, I am vairy sorry.

You see: I won't let myself be downcast.

So I went home early instead, to find the children cooped up in front of the television – on such a fine evening – while out in the garden, under the apple tree, were Max Kennerly and Kate, already drinking at six-thirty and looking more than a little conspiratorial. As there were also tea-things uncleared away they must have been discussing something very deeply. But what? As soon as Max had gone Kate busied herself tidying up and organizing the children and starting on the supper. In answer to my queries she said impatiently that Sue Kennerly had been in town on some errand with the daughter while Max had been lecturing in Shrivenham. Coming straight home and finding an empty house he had invited himself to tea.

'What were you talking about so intently?'

'*Nothing*. And if you can't help, at least don't get in my way!'

As you may imagine, the suspicion leaped to mind that they might have been discussing yours truly. Had word filtered back of a certain Three-Litre calling in the Beechway? It would be too ironic if my perfectly innocent call on your mother had been misconstrued. But Kate is usually unequivocal when I am the object of her wrath!

After the children had gone to bed she did volunteer something about Max being worried about his future. Apparently he is forty-nine, and unless he is given a new appointment next year he will be retired. On half-pay it will not be easy to keep two boys at public school and that surly daughter at her so-called university.

September 19

More and more mysterious! Last night it was Sue Kennerly and dear Kate closeted together, again with drinks, again with a litter of tea things, plus a certain redness of the eye on Sue's part. What is going on?

When I challenged Kate she said, 'I can't tell you. I've promised. So please don't ask me.'

September 22

All is revealed! And such a revelation that I feel compelled to drop by and pass it on to you straightaway, whoever may be there. After all, you and Geoffrey both met her and even your mother may have heard mention of her. It's Sarah Kennerly, the daughter – she was at our dinner party that time; hardly spoke, just sighed and looked contemptuous. I told you about this so-called university she attends and the long-haired riff-raff she is in the habit of bringing home.

Well, she spent the long vac with one of them in a kibbutz, if you please, and to cut a long story short – if you haven't guessed already – she's pregnant.

Apparently she ran out of supplies of the Pill and didn't know how to go about replacing them in Israel, or more likely couldn't be bothered. The only thing that surprises me is that she wants to have the child, and not 'get rid of it', in the callous phrase of the day. I suppose that reflects some credit on her, though it would reflect even more – and certainly indicate more consideration for others – if she would agree to get married.

Oh, they propose to live together when they return to the university, if they haven't been doing so already. Moreover, the fellow is said to be willing to marry her; it is Sarah who has the modish ideas about independence and not shackling herself to bourgeois institutions, etcetera. It seems there are also financial advantages in that two single grants come to more than one married one. When I reflect that single or double it comes out of the taxpayer's and ratepayer's pocket I must confess I see red. I can guess what Geoffrey would have to say!

Kate, rather to my surprise, is far more tolerant. 'Suppose it were Janet – or Miranda! What then?' I demanded.

'As it may well be, when their time comes,' she replied in her most infuriatingly calm way.

'In which case they will have five minutes to pack their things, get out and never show their faces again.'

'My goodness, we *are* the stern parent.'

'Just as well someone is.'

'Look; they are our dearest girls. We are bringing them up as sensibly and imaginatively as we can – better than I was brought up. But when they're eighteen or nineteen they'll go their own ways, and there's nothing we can do about it except trust them. Sarah Kennerly has been silly but she's still a sweetie, and she loves that Roger What's-his-name. It's not the end of the world.'

Hmmm. I couldn't help wondering if she would be as understanding of certain other trespasses, if she knew of them!

Poor Sue is the one I feel sorry for. I expect she had all the usual dreams of her daughter making a good match. Max has accepted everything with his usual equanimity.

To tell the truth I find him hard to understand. One would expect a soldier to behave in more soldierly fashion. A little firmer discipline and the whole sorry situation need never have come about. He rather reminds me of the troops who have been sent to Northern Ireland to deal with the damned trouble-makers there, and whose task, as far as one can tell, is to be shot at but never shoot back. All weekend one heard him playing the piano, and not even Beethoven or Chopin any more, only this weird plonking music of his.

September 23

Sorry if I didn't tell you as much about Sarah Kennerly as you would have liked last night. I know it is just the story to interest a woman and indeed I rehearsed a very full account on the way to you. Perhaps the one drawback of this recording habit is that one is sometimes deceived into thinking one has passed on some news when one has only committed it to magnetic tape.

Besides, the discovery that your mother had at last gone back to Poole drove everything else from my head! I'll do my best to make amends this evening, if I decide to call. The main development since yesterday is that the happy couple are to be married after all, having discovered that because of Max's income the girl has only been receiving a limited grant and that they may after all be better off as a wedded couple. What a fairy-tale romance! The ceremony is to take place at the registry office just before the term begins at the university, with a small reception *chez* Kennerly afterwards. We are, of course, invited. I can't help thinking how poor Sue must have looked forward to a white wedding for her daughter at some fashionable military chapel with a guard of honour brandishing their swords to make a triumphal arch, and then a glittering reception at White's or Boodle's.

As it is, Kate talks of a new outfit for the occasion. Perhaps it is just as well we are spared the full panoply.

Incidentally, the circumstances of the episode rather lead me to wonder if you are adequately armed against the vagaries of nature. In this day of pills and permanent devices, etcetera, we men have rather got into the habit of leaving it to the ladies. I must remember to check this point with you.

September 30

Veronica Hart has delivered the manuscript of *Stanley the Suburban Squirrel* and on the whole we're very pleased with it. There are some points of style and grammar I shall have to correct, plus not a few spelling mistakes, I'm afraid. Also, later chapters have a certain playful quality – notably in an episode involving a tom-cat who falls foul of the squirrels – which I am not sure is entirely suitable for young readers. However, Walter sees no objection and is anxious to get the typesetting in hand as soon as possible, with a view to publication in the spring.

I must say the illustrations Veronica has furnished are delightful. It is most amusing to see how she has caught the very essence of Mr Smailes the demon developer in 'Mr Bodger the Builder', who is the villain in the story. There is likewise a cleric called the Revd. Grouch who bears a distinct resemblance to old Lumsden. I dare say you will be able to identify one or two more of the two-legged characters from your experience of the Beechway!

Apropos of which, though it was great fun to meet Mollie Fox-Rogers again the other evening, it was slightly disconcerting when she came in through the french windows with no more warning than a 'Coooee, it's me.' Though we were luckily not in any awkward situation I thought I detected a speculative look in her eye. If we are to continue these pleasant moments of relaxation, I wonder if you couldn't drop a hint to her that neighbourliness can be taken too far. I really can't afford to be the victim of idle gossip just when we are launched on our publishing venture.

As I have the precious manuscript with me for Kate to see, I think I had better not look in this evening. I would feel uneasy leaving it in the car right along the road there, and if I brought it into your house I might forget it, which would never do!

Chapter Eight

Will the summer last forever? Each morning I look out of the window anxiously. Already the mornings are becoming autumnal, with a light mist and a smell of woodsmoke. The beech trees are starting to turn and the ferns on the heath are quite golden. But by the time I set off for the office the sun is as bright as ever. If only one weren't so busy, but Mrs Cernik is on holiday with her tiresome daughter, Walter is tied up at Grosvenor House and I must get *Stanley* off to the printers.

Veronica came to the office this morning to work with me on the corrections and marking-up. Apparently she has had experience of copy-editing. Though she disagreed violently with my emendations, by standing firm in some instances and giving way in others I was able to ensure we made good progress. That is the art of life, is it not? She was wearing her new contact lenses and I must say the transformation is remarkable. One suddenly perceives that she is a very pretty girl with a nice figure. Even her off-hand manner had disappeared in the vehemence of our discussion.

Unfortunately she is not yet used to the contact lenses

105

and her eyes began to water painfully after a couple of hours – you would know about such teething troubles. As she had confidently left her thick pebble-glasses at home she proposed we should adjourn there for a working lunch and afterwards finish the task. I wasn't too happy about this, especially as I could not help wishing I was being whisked not merely to the murky Thames somewhere by Lots Road power station but out of oppressive London altogether and on my way to a rendezvous by clear waters, amid trees and grass.

Which said, she drove her little Fiat through the traffic with great verve – the coincidence that yours, Kate's and hers should be identical models still amazes me. And guess what? The squalid houseboat I had imagined was far from the truth. One trod one's way gingerly across the decks of several shabby properties before reaching hers, which occupies what is presumably a favoured position farthest from the shore and next to the open river, but her vessel proved to be a converted sailing barge, very roomy and beautifully fitted out with modern kitchen, 'fridge, electric light, telephone, hi-fi and, if you can believe it, colour television! She told me she had paid some thousands of pounds for it and was now also looking for a cottage in the country. She produced smoked salmon for lunch and, though only taking Coca-Cola herself, opened a bottle of wine that I don't mind saying was rather better than we can normally afford to drink. Add in the little Fiat, and one wonders just how much she can be earning at the tender age of twenty-two or three. Our advance was hardly in that class, unless Walter increased it unbeknown to me.

I couldn't help wondering if perhaps she were not . . . all on her own. One had never associated her with anything like that. Indeed, up till this moment one had thought of her only as a rather frumpy girl. But when the telephone rang, as it did several times, she spoke once of 'we' and another time said something about 'Tom' being in Ireland. There was such a clutter of stuff in the little bathroom, and such a profusion of magazines, drawings, books lying around, not to mention large photographs pinned up everywhere, that it was impossible to tell if there were any exclusively male belongings.

There *was* a full-size bed, covered with a patchwork quilt.

But why am I bothering you with all this? Wasn't Geoffrey due to be playing in the first round of the Captain's Prize this evening? One might drop by.

You have never said what you think of my moustache. I wonder if it is rather 'square', as they say these days.

October 3

No, I am not in the least annoyed by what happened last night. It was perfectly understandable that with Geoffrey out as usual, you should take advantage of my happening to drop by and ask me if I could do something about the overflow from the upstairs cistern. Nothing is more distracting than the ceaseless drip of water in the yard outside, not to mention the damp patch it can make, and normally, of course it is a simple job to change the washer. Normally, however, one knows where to turn the mains off. Attempting to do it before we had succeeded in locating the stopcock was idiotic. I'm sorry if I got a bit grumpy but how was I going to explain a soaking wet shirt to Kate? All very well your offering to lend me one of Geoffrey's, there were still obvious dangers. Luckily Kate didn't notice, being too occupied with wedding preparations next door, and I've hidden it now until I can return it. Looking back, it was just another of our hilarious mishaps. If I've learned anything from you, Mrs Davies, it is a sense of the ridiculous! I only wish I could have seen the humorous side this time as quickly as you did, and not stumped off as I did.

It is interesting, incidentally, that both you and Kate should find my misgivings about *Stanley* a bit 'stuffy'. Perhaps I am a little over-sensitive.

I suppose you'll be expecting to hear all about the wedding. Well, I'll do my best, but the difficulty – if you remember – is that if I put it on to this machine first it becomes rather boring to recount it all again, and if I don't I probably forget half the details. As it is, we really don't have enough time to relax at all if cisterns are going to overflow or that wretched Fox-Rogers woman to breeze in and out as she pleases.

Besides, I can't be late this evening, as Max and Sue are coming to take pot luck. It was Kate's idea. She guessed they might be feeling a little flat now that it's all over and they haven't even the flurry of activity to distract them from the second-bestness of the occasion. Not that Max seems to have been unduly disturbed by having to preside over the wedding feast of expectant bride and unsavoury, nihilistic groom.

One vignette, I thought, summed up everything I find baffling about one whose career, after all, has been dedicated to example and leadership. As we arrived at that house after the registry office ceremony the semblance of a pukka reception took shape. I dare say it was quite unplanned, knowing Max. The tables had been laid out in the garden, with our Mrs Wild and their Mrs Jones hovering at the ready plus a very smart army chap in a white tunic who was pouring the champagne. Max and Sue naturally took their places just outside the french windows, along with the bride and groom, and as we filed out on to the lawn we made our formal congratulations, etcetera, if with fingers crossed!

Sporting a flower in his buttonhole and exuding

bonhomie, Max was looking as proud a father as if Sarah had just married the Prince of Wales in Westminster Abbey. I saw him give her a big squeeze and she flashed back the sort of smile which I suppose one terms 'radiant'. To tell the truth I feel rather better disposed towards her than formerly. When it was my turn to kiss her she gave me such a grin and, I swear, the suspicion of a wink. Do you think she did recognize us in the pub that day?

Even the 'lucky man' whom I must start to call Roger, I suppose, seemed marginally more acceptable. His hair had been trimmed and for once he was wearing a reasonably orthodox suit. His parents were there – perfectly respectable if hardly very interesting; the father is in local government, I believe. And Roger is rather clever, one now learns; taking a doctorate in some fashionable subject. But his best man was a real shocker. Can you imagine? – he had actually turned up on this rather special day wearing, you know, one of those native nightshirt things, a caftan, or whatever it is. Not to mention hair frizzed out like a Hottentot's and a liberal bedecking of beads and bangles!

Which brings me to my vignette. It so happened that Kate and I had got slightly separated as we waited to go through. She was deep in conversation with Sarah's godfather, who is a senior colleague of Max's, a major-general and, if one may say so, much more of a military figure. What he thought of it all I hesitate to imagine. Kate went first, then the General, then if you please – pushing his way shamelessly in front of me – this hideous Best Man.

Max can't have planned his response. It must have been quite spontaneous. On Kate he planted a most affectionate kiss, indeed on the mouth rather than the cheek. For the General he drew himself up to his full height and threw a mock salute, in itself a rather extraordinary gesture. To the Best Man he inclined forward as if in Oriental greeting, head bent to hands pressed together in peace.

Following on, I had myself to be content with an impish smile and a conventional handshake, though no less warm a welcome, I hope.

I don't think anyone else fully noticed. Kate certainly hadn't when I asked her later. I had the impression no one was meant to notice, it was a purely private joke for Max's own . . . consolation? I just don't know.

The reception thereafter was jolly pleasant, I must say. The champagne flowed, there was an excellent meal to which we sat down, rather as in those *al fresco* wedding feasts you see in foreign films. The Best Man proposed the couple's health in not too offensive a manner; there was even some laughter; Roger replied not too graciously.

The wedding presents were informally displayed in the drawing-room, among them the set of non-stick saucepans from Kate and I. But guess what the Best Man had somehow brought along, and which people were foolishly exclaiming over? A great old iron cooking pot. You know, the type of thing the witches sit around in *Macbeth*. What are they supposed to be? Cannibals?

Such a fine, warm afternoon when we're well into October was a delight, of course, but it left me feeling a little sad, I'm not sure why. I felt I was lacking something or someone, and that life was slipping by all too quickly. After the General had left yesterday, Max played the piano all afternoon, that plonking music of his in which even the individual notes seem lonely, so separated are they from each other. I noticed that Kate also seemed to grow pensive as she listened.

Why don't we have that picnic without more ado? It has been a vague dream too long. Soon the weather *must* break. Already the mornings are cool and the leaves begin to fall. I will be able to tell you all about the wedding, at infinite leisure. There will be no interruptions to fear, we can be as

110

relaxed as Adam and Eve in the Garden of Eden. Let's say Wednesday, the day after tomorrow. That is still your free afternoon, isn't it? And I have more time at last. Mrs Cernik is back from her holiday. Did I mention that Veronica Hart has gone off to Spain?

October 7

Good: then it is all arranged for tomorrow. I shall meet you at the Reindeer Hotel on the Walford road and I will lead the way from there. I discreetly established in conversation with Max last night that the club house is closed again except at the weekends and some evenings. Already many of the boats have been laid up for the winter – Max took his out of the water before the boys went back to Oundle. The spot I have in mind is in any case some distance from the centre of things. There is a rough track, dating from gravel-extraction days, I imagine, which leads towards a little 'beach' I have several times noticed from the water. It looks to be clean and quite secluded.

I have rather enjoyed planning the operation. Into the boot of the Three-Litre I have already smuggled a large old rug and two towels – no swimming costumes, though! Also a bottle of wine and our picnic basket with plastic cutlery and glasses, etcetera. Sun-tan oil, however absurd that may sound in October; better safe than sorry. And tomorrow I shall buy rolls, butter, ham, cheese, fruit, whatever offers, not forgetting a packet of your usual cigarettes and a box of matches. See: I forget nothing.

The afternoon seemed as warm as ever in London.

October 9

It was no one's fault. When I threw the bedroom window open to do my exercises – one likes to keep in trim, even if the effort was to go unappreciated on this occasion – I had a suspicion the day had started too brightly. Instead of the morning mist of late there was a lively breeze stirring the fallen leaves. Still, the sun was shining and I whistled blithely as I shaved.

'You're full of the joys of spring,' Kate observed.

'Of autumn,' I corrected her.

'I wish it *would* hurry up and be autumn. Trudging round the shops yesterday trying to find a bra for Janet I was as hot and melty as if it were August still. When is this summer going to end?'

'Don't say that,' I wailed.

Yes, it is absurd: a brassiere at twelve years old. It is not even as if she had any need for one, simply that her school friends have started to wear them, so she must. I expect you've been through all this with Rebecca. By the way, you can't really have expected me to remember what everyone wore at the wedding. Apart from the fact that mere man is traditionally unobservant in such respects, I've always assumed you were a cut above the empty-headed preoccupation with clothes and fashions of the conventional housewife. Kate had this very elegant suit, I think you'd call it, in silky stuff with a pattern of tiny flowers, though normally she delights in her long floaty skirts in summer time. She had the idea, quite unfounded, that her legs don't suit the 'mini'.

Apropos of which, I admit I had forgotten that as a smart receptionist you would be wearing a smart town outfit, complete with frilly blouse and high heels. I've got so used to you in the cool casuals you substitute at home. True, I had to pop into the office to check on the correspondence before buzzing off to do the rounds of some booksellers – as Mrs Cernik was led to understand! – and was myself in business attire, but I had planned to shed jacket and tie before we met in order to set the right mood. I didn't do so

112

simply because the Reindeer was a rather posher place than I had imagined.

It was a good idea to have a quick drink before moving off. I could hardly carry around the makings of a good gin-and-tonic, with ice and lemon. I agree that the restaurant menu looked, and smelled, extremely inviting. We must certainly try it another time. But I had bought all that liver sausage and Bel Paese and the rolls and the pears, which incidentally the man swore were ready for eating, you simply can't trust anyone these days. The whole idea was to have a picnic, or had you forgotten that? Also, I did suggest in a small voice that there was no need to take two cars on, we could have left your little Fiat in the carpark and retrieved it later. That way you would never have had to take it along the track, which I warned you was rough.

If I didn't mention the digger thing that was working the other side of the trees it was because I had no idea they'd started taking gravel from that particular site again. Max said nothing about it. Nor was I to know you don't like liver pâté. I honestly think some of your complaints were niggling. You used to have such a sense of humour. The main thing was that the place was perfectly secluded, just as I had hoped, and very pleasant in the sunshine as long as one was sheltered from the wind. You needed little urging from me to divest yourself of those inappropriate outer garments.

What we might have done, I now see, was to have a swim straightaway. On the other hand it was after half-past one and we were both hungry. I must say I enjoyed the repast. Even wine seems to taste better out in the open. Perhaps if you hadn't smoked between mouthfuls you might have enjoyed it more. If you don't mind my saying so, you were rather over-reacting to the presence of a few midges, which in any case vanished as soon as the sun went in.

Nor did I 'chivvy' you into going for a dip. I merely

113

reminded you that it had been one of the objects of the outing. No one could have been more surprised when you said, 'All right, if that's what you want then,' and suddenly sprang into action. I was just about to follow suit when you dived – or as you put it afterwards went 'A over T' on the mud. Which was just as well, because at this very moment I became aware of the tipper lorry bouncing towards us from the trees. Standing in the back were a couple of young labourers who were cheering and making crude gestures, but luckily the driver took no notice and gaining the track, drove away.

Thereafter I was fully occupied with helping you ashore and getting a towel wrapped round you, just as the first squall struck. What icy rain! I felt every bit as invigorated afterwards as I had been swimming myself.

I thought I did well to have everything packed by the time you'd dressed. Sorry about that sticky mud, but it will brush off when it's dry. There was some on my trousers. The flat tyre on your little Fiat was a blow, I admit. I would have managed to change the wheel single-handed while you sheltered in my car if only the nuts hadn't been so ridiculously tight. They put them on with these big spanners in the garage and expect you to get them off with the tinny little wheel-brace provided in the car.

Yes, I will arrange for Dino to fix your tyre and check the silencer where you think it hit a bump, though I am sure that if you went along on spec. he would be only too happy to oblige. I really think that famous sense of humour of yours deserted you on this occasion. While I forced myself to see the funny side. It must have made their day, those chaps in the tipper lorry!

Of course, at the time I couldn't help feeling a distinct sense of anti-climax. It was early for me to go home. Besides, I had to do something positive, retrieve something from the wreckage. I went to the bookshop in Eton, and one in Slough, and had a word with the respective managers about *It's Fun*. They seemed quite receptive. Crossing Dorney Common afterwards the rain was slanting down. On the heath the leaves were whirling from the trees. After supper I made a fire in the sitting-room.

Chapter Nine

The first of the month, which I often use as a kind of minor New Year's Day, the spur to make a start on something I've been meaning to do for some time, or in this case resume something: namely these confidences.

It is Sunday. Kate and the children have been at a children's party all afternoon. I played the whole of the recordings made up until last October, when on an impulse I brought the gadget in from the car and hid it in the safe, I'm not sure why.

I must say I was rather horrified. So pompous. Not very kind. And absolutely no sense of humour! There were really some priceless things that happened to one. Or rather, to me. It's a funny thing about using 'one' instead of 'I' – one does actually think of oneself as a kind of third party one is cleaning up and presenting to the world. 'I' is more honest.

I have just played back the foregoing. It sounds quite different from the me that was. But is it merely the style that has changed? Am I myself any more honest than oneself was? I am still the same Graham Godley, married to the same Kate Godley, and she hasn't noticed anything as far as I know. On the other hand I've just remembered that I had a moustache until I shaved it off last Christmas. I'd quite forgotten I ever had one. I bet she has, too.

The main thing is that I now have a new recipient for these wafflings.

March 2

The first copies of *Stanley the Suburban Squirrel* have arrived from the binders. One is on its way to you, another sits on the seat right by me. I have only to drop my eyes to see the cover which Gilvray Ryman designed from your drawings. Sammy grins cheekily from the scaffolding of a half-built house, a biscuit between his front paws, while below him angry Mr Bodger the Builder waves his fist. In the background a tree is being chopped down, which, as I explained to Mrs Cernik, instantly establishes the theme of the book.

'Are such creatures eating cookies?' she objected. I think she can't ever have been a child herself. As a matter of fact that's been half the trouble with our *It's Fun* titles. We've had several reactions from the trade to the effect that old Applebee's illustrations are just too good for young readers, especially one that shows little field mice being digested. If I had my way you would take over the series. Still, there's Stanley II to keep us occupied. Have you thought of a title yet? I wondered about *Stanley at the Barricades*? Seriously, Walter and I are working very hard to develop a topical board-game about the situation in Ulster. Foybells want to rush it out for next season, if possible. At least we are so far spared the annual wrangle with Zillah Graves over the Mugwumps, bread and butter of our business, as she and her appalling husband have been in Australia since Christmas. If I'm rambling, well it must be nearly six months since I last used this thing and you know, it's not easy to get back into the routine.

Actually, I was addressing someone else then. Since you ask – or would if you could – yes, it was a woman. I'll tell you about her as we go along. I used to tell her about you. Well, not in the same way. I only told her about you when you were a girl in thick glasses who was doing a book for us. I had no inkling . . . no, that's not strictly true, either. I mean, the first time you set eyes on someone about whom you're going to have a thing, it must register although you don't realize it straightaway. It wasn't until you came into the office that day with your new contact lenses and your hair tied back in a pony-tail that I realized – no, not even then. Not until after that, when I found myself trying to hold on to the day, just as in childhood I used to try and hold on to magic days, like Christmas or Whipsnade or when my father took me to the Air Display and we went up, in an Airspeed Ferry actually. Days I wanted never to become yesterdays.

But you went off to Spain and North Africa and whole weeks went by. Once I drove home via World's End and Fulham instead of the Cromwell Road. It was getting dark. At last there had been heavy rain, and the river was brown and turbulent. Though there were no lights showing and I know it was pointless, I picked my way across the intervening decks and stood on yours. Through the porthole I could just pick out the patchwork quilt on the bed. Such a nostalgia filled me for the few hours we took to have lunch and talk our way through the text of *Stanley*.

I daresay it was autumn making me gloomy. It is Kate's favourite season but far from mine. Things are dying. Those that survive are getting older. We went for a picnic, this friend and I, which went horribly wrong because it just happened to be the exact moment when last summer fell off plop like an over-ripe plum and autumn – practically winter – came whistling in. Actually, I was all for settling for a pub lunch instead, especially as she was all dolled up in a suit

118

and flouncy blouse and high heels. She was working as a receptionist for some optician, curiously the same firm that you went to, Broadbents. Incidentally, I think you're quite right not to keep on with the contacts if they are not comfortable. It's all very well for Tom to cry 'persevere'. He doesn't have to wear the wretched things. Besides, I think spectacles on a girl can be very sexy.

Rather to my surprise, though, she was determined to go ahead with the picnic. She is a bit of a sun-worshipper and would have envied you those weeks in Spain and Africa. The sun was still shining when we got to the place, which is over Walford way by some water, and she was down to her pants and bra in no time. There were even a few midges, until the wind turned colder. Then just as we were going to have a swim – well first of all, a tipper lorry came bouncing along full of yelling workers and immediately afterwards a squall of icy rain! On top of that she got a puncture in her little Fiat, same as yours, which I had to mend before we could cut our losses and flee. Luckily I could see the funny side.

Brrrr!

But now it will soon be spring again. Across the heath the bare trees have a very faint green fuzz to them, almost like a mould, which in fact is the first little buds showing. The snowdrops are out in the garden, the crocuses spiking up. And just as nature has been working away beneath the snow and frost, ready to burst into flower, so *Stanley* was quietly taking shape in remote printing works. As the proofs arrived while Walter was at Harrogate I was privileged to telephone and tell you. Should I drop a set in on you on my way home?

Boringly, you said you were coming up to Long Acre anyway, you would call and pick them up. How bustling and busy you were. Stayed only long enough for a bitter lemon – I must ask Mrs Cernik to get in some Coca-Cola –

then buttoned up that long Hussar coat and put on that fur hat and wound that striped scarf round your neck and said you must be on your way. It was during the cold spell in January.

'In you sweep,' I said, 'like Anna Karenina. Have us running round after you, then sweep out again!' But you laughed, which was something I had never seen you do before, and you looked at me with a directness, a sort of speculation, that was also new.

'I'm sorry,' you said. 'But honestly, I've got to go into *Rave*, they're waiting for the piece.'

'Of course,' I said. 'Anyway, I've got New York coming through on the phone any minute.' Perhaps I even had! – I don't remember.

More weeks went by, until one day in you popped again, returning the corrected proofs. I didn't tell you that we had long since marked a set and sent them back. But what more natural than to make a date for lunch and sort out some ideas for a *Stanley* sequel? What more natural to anyone but Mrs Cernik, that is? Her eyes glistened like humbugs as you left. Because she's mittel-European she assumes she is endowed with special insight into the human heart, which means in practice that she's either sighing sentimentally over Kate's and my married bliss or leaping to the conclusion I'm carrying on unworthily. That's why I called after you, you must come out and see us at the heath again. And so you must. Kate would be thrilled, I know.

'Ow old that Veronica?' Mrs Cernik demanded, putting on her most knowing expression.

'Twenty-three, twenty-four, something like that.'

'Hmm.'

I knew what she was driving at all right. So I can give you the – the best part of twenty years. What of it?

And then – well, if old Tantalus who gave his name to 'tantalize' had been staked out there in the Thames, dying of thirst with his tongue three inches from the surface, even he would have sympathized. 'We can meet near your end of the world, if you like,' I said on the phone, which apart from being a play on 'World's End' which I don't think you registered, was a practical consideration: why should you always have to flog up to Baker Street, unless you have somewhere else to go, of course? It's in our interest to keep you at typewriter and drawing board.

The old Le Provençal hadn't changed much since my gay Earls Court days with Affiliated Newspapers, as was, except for the prices. I should have remembered about the garlic because Kate is super-sensitive about these things; sometimes I think there must have been a werewolf in her family. When I let slip it was you I had been lunching, however, she was mollified. What did I tell you? Also, their carafes of vino are a full litre and if I had known you were going to stick to Coca-Cola I would have ordered a *demi* only.

But it was very pleasant. Suddenly we got on like a house on fire, and a lot of amusing *Stanley* ideas emerged. When old Gaston asked if you wanted coffee and you said not unless I did, that was just what I had been hoping! You could perhaps rustle up a cup of tea, I suggested, if we went back to the boat and got a few of the ideas down on paper straightaway.

Outside there was wintry sunlight but it was also cold again. As we walked to where you had left your car I realized that I should have darted into the Gents before we left. I'm always forgetting! As we threaded our way down to the river, oh dear! Every set of traffic lights seemed to turn to red just as we approached. I can't imagine what I was making in the way of conversation. My attention was focused on only one thing. When we reached the moorings I'm afraid I hurried willy-nilly across the various decks ahead of you. Alas, the door was locked and you were still hunting for your keys. There was nothing for it but excuse myself and duck behind the superstructure and reinforce old Father Thames! Some chaps waved as they chugged by on a coal barge.

What shame but what relief! Down in the galley you were very sympathetic. Some I know would only have laughed. 'Now,' you said, filling the kettle, 'what would you like?' As I didn't reply at once you added, 'Tea or coffee?'

I hadn't prepared my reply, however studied it may have sounded. I can still hear myself saying it in a funny formal voice. 'What I most want,' I said, 'probably isn't available.'

'What's that?' And I think you knew what I was going to say.

'You.'

There was such a silence I thought you must be cross.

I said, 'Now you're cross. I'm sorry but it was the truth.'

'No,' you said. 'It's not that. I've always fancied you, too. It's just that Tom may come back any moment now. Actually, I thought he might be back already.'

'Oh, Tom,' I said, feeling very cast down. 'He lives here then?'

You turned on the Calor gas and struck a match. 'Off and on.'

'Doesn't he have a job?'

'He's a photographer.'

'Oh, one of those. Are you sure he'll be back? I mean, soon?'

'I can't be sure he won't. He was only going to the pub for lunch, he said.' And then you went on, in just the same voice – but it was as if trumpets sounded – 'He's supposed to be going to Vietnam and Cambodia and places next month, if you can wait till then.'

Just couldn't I, if that was the only way! I made a chart on my blotter at the office, a square crossed off every day and three on Mondays. Only seven left! What's more, as an earnest of good intentions – or should I say 'bad intentions'? – at least we kissed and caressed after we'd carried two mugs of hasty, weak tea into the big room or whatever you call it, an eye apiece on the deck outside and the chafing, bumping bridge of boats between us and shore.

'Married men,' you said as if playing with the idea of withdrawing the offer, 'I'm not sure about married men. I've only had an affair with one married man before. I mean, there's that nice what-was-her name to think of?'

'Kate, and you don't have to worry about her, honestly. She likes you.'

How avid were your kisses.

And then you said, out of the blue, 'I wonder what you look like without your clothes.'

Should I have leaped up and cried, 'I'll show you'? Or said, 'More to the point, what do you look like?' (I know you will be beautiful.) Instead I said rather foolishly, 'It's not really the weather for nothing on.' Could have bitten off my tongue. But you didn't mind, just answered the objection practically. 'I don't know,' you said. 'It's quite cosy in front of an electric fire.'

You see: when a girl says that to a man twenty years older than she is, he can't help being flattered. Seven days to go!

March 4

Tantalus looms again! – and on home ground. Will I be able to bear it? Admittedly I had suggested your coming for a weekend but I had no idea Kate would respond so soon. Tom is therefore invited too.

123

Meanwhile Walter wants us to press ahead with the *Belfast Barricades* game while Foybells are still keen. The trouble is that the situation in Ulster is changing all the time. Up till last year it would have been a straightforward civil rights issue, with the object of the game to win various political changes, etcetera – which would have been purely for adults, and not so many of those. Now it is potentially much more exciting, of course, with bombs and water cannon and 'no-go' areas and so on. But as we learned from *Hawks and Doves* and even more from *Sabra*, players do not always like having to act the part of particular powers. Nobody wants to be the Arabs! Sometimes it's better to have the competition between rival groups fighting the same enemy.

I said that the Official and the Provisional wings of the IRA were just the groups with whom young people would be able to identify quite willingly. In addition you could have the Socialists, whatever they call themselves, and perhaps the more enlightened Protestants, which would take care of any strong religious feelings amongst customers. Walter objects that this casts the British Army as the enemy. As a naturalized Briton he is extra-patriotic, of course, but he has a point. I must ask Max.

What we need to do most is some concentrated cool thinking and that's the last thing I can manage these days, what with the suspense and everything. Six days now.

Zillah Graves and her husband are back from Australia, so that's Walter distracted, too.

March 9

Kate said, 'Do we put them in the same room?' Actually there is only one spare room but at the cost of some wear and tear on everyone's nerves we can move Little Sam in

124

with the girls on a put-u-up, and that leaves another single room.

I said, 'What did Sue do with Sarah and what's-his-name – Roger? Before they were married, that is?'

'That was different.' Then she made up her mind in that imperious way of hers. 'If you say they're living together of course they'll expect to share. That's settled, then.'

What could I do but nod agreement, however galling the prospect? At least it meant that your arrival was free from awkward hesitation as we tried to find out what you were expecting. 'Graham will show you your room,' Kate said firmly, 'while I do the last-minute things to the meal' – by the way, don't worry about having been a bit late; before the children started to arrive we often didn't have lunch until two; it is just that they sometimes get fractious if they're too hungry.

We had hoped they would accept you as a couple without further question. Unfortunately there was this wedding next door which left the girls, particularly, very interested in the whole subject. Also, I'm afraid Miranda does like to stir things up, though referring to you as 'Veruca' was a perfectly innocent mistake, she's a character in *Charlie and the Chocolate Factory* which they all love so. I'm sure you know it. Anyway, what was that she came out with so bluntly to Tom? 'Is Veruca your mummy – I mean, your wife?'

'In a way,' said Kate quickly, 'And it's *Veronica*.'

'Did you have a lot of nice things?' asked Janet. She was very taken with all the presents Sarah Kennerly had.

'No,' said Tom, very neatly I thought, 'you see we haven't had the party yet when people bring you presents.'

Then trust Little Sam to pipe up with what I had been dreading. 'Do you put your seed in her?' he asked. You know, this was the way Kate used to explain it to them – she held very firmly that the children should be given plain

125

answers to their questions the minute they became interested in sex and how babies were born and so on. No nonsense about gooseberry bushes or the doctor's little bag.

Never mind, the episode passed without too many red faces. Tom roared with laughter. I must say I liked him a lot. Once you get used to his very contemporary style of speech he's most amusing, and of course he had been to so many unusual places. Vietnam, Borneo, Cape Canaveral, Russia, the Congo. As I couldn't resist saying to Kate as we went to bed, to think that next week he will be right across the world in Vietnam! All she said was that she hoped he would remember to send us copies of the photographs he took on the heath in the afternoon. She can never have enough pictures of the children and frankly I'm no David Bailey – is it? – when it comes to using a camera.

Sorry about imposing the Kennerlys on you at dinner. It was Kate's idea to ask them. They are our only neighbours, of course, but I could see that someone a little nearer your own ages might have been more fun. And although they have this daughter we were telling you about, who married her fellow somewhat suddenly, well – Sue especially can be a bit wearing. Kate has a theory that her loud voice goes automatically with being a service wife: the higher in rank the husband rises, the more loudly she feels she has to address the wives of his juniors. Max, I hoped, would be interested in some of the wars that Tom has covered, but he has never been one to talk much of his trade. Not until Northern Ireland was mentioned did he rise to the bait, so to speak – as you will hardly need reminding. I'm sorry if Tom got rather sternly challenged over his perfectly reasonable criticisms of the army's activities there. I've noticed before that for all Max's benign exterior it doesn't take much to bring a flash of the military man beneath. When I mentioned the Belfast barricade game which Walter and I are working on, which by the way, we're thinking of calling *Urban Guerilla*, it was my turn to be put in my place!

'That should be fun for the family,' was all he said, but the tone was pretty icy.

Of course he is worried just now about his future. He has spent some time lately scouting out possible jobs when he retires. The trouble is that he has no qualifications. Apparently the army offered to send him to Cambridge at one time and he couldn't be bothered. I must say I find it hard to be very sympathetic. Now they publish those tables of earnings in the recruiting advertisements you can see exactly what someone like Max is getting for sitting in an office a few hours each day, and as Tom pointed out after they'd gone, all out of our pockets. If he's still going to get half of that for doing absolutely nothing, I can't see it's a tragedy. He and Sue could save fifteen hundred a year straightaway by taking their great boys away from Oundle and sending them to our grammar school. You should hear Kate on the subject of state versus private education!

Sunday morning we *wanted* you to have a long lie-in. Kate likes to take the children to church for, oh, various complex reasons. But I'm only too glad of an excuse to stay behind and make some toast or brew fresh coffee if anyone comes down. I was just glancing through the review sections to make sure they haven't run their children's book specials yet – obviously we're hoping to time Stanley's debut to coincide – when I heard the plumbing upstairs. Popped up to see if you wanted anything, if it was you, and was rewarded with a delicious vision tripping along the landing in long white nighty, that heavy, glossy hair cascading over your shoulders.

'Ready for some breakfast?' I called. Was I right to read a bit of extra meaning into that complicit smile and reply of 'Super'? Only three days to go. If it makes me sound callous I can't help it, but I was also checking in the papers to make

127

sure the situation hadn't resolved itself in South East Asia and thus made unnecessary a certain ace photographer's journey. Anyway, it was a nice suggestion Kate had left with me that you and Tom and I take Rastus across the heath for a Sunday morning drink at the Browsden Arms, and she would join us as soon as she'd organized the lunch and we could all drive back.

I love these first sunny intimations of spring, with all the promise of the good months to come. Rastus bounded about like a two-year-old. I thought how well you strode out, how well you carried yourself. It's important, you know. I can't stand these round-shouldered girls you see slopping along. The pub is – well, yes, Tom sensed it at once. He's quite right. It was such a characterful little place, a real earth-man's ale-house, until that fellow Charles bought it and tarted it up. The one in the plum-coloured blazer who was holding court.

You could sup draught beer from the wood instead of that fizzy stuff that made Tom pull a face. The old boy would fill your pot from a barrel on a trestle, a real taste of old England if a little flat now and then. But I'm forgetting: you're mostly a soft drinks girl. Anyway, it's all vodka-and-tonic and Campari-soda now, as being consumed by that loud-voiced bunch over by the bar. Tom immediately got their measure again. 'Wife-swappers holding their Sunday morning post-mortem?' he said in a stage whisper. The fellow in the blazer who held his elbow out at right-angles when he lifted his glass was Patrick Somebody who was in the Navy, and the blonde with the awful laugh was Mollie Fox-Rogers. But Binnie, the one who came over to see us and whom you said you remembered from the fête last year – well, I always think she's a cut above the rest. If her rotten husband wasn't always on the golf course I'm sure she wouldn't bother with that crowd. She was at St Andrews U. at the same time as I was – well, part of the time, that is. She was out in Africa for a spell, which perhaps dried out her skin and left it looking a bit older than she really is. As Tom said afterwards, though, still quite a fine figure of a woman.

Actually, that wasn't the most tactful of remarks, Kate having arrived and found us apparently forming a cosy foursome without her. 'There you are,' she said, and 'Oh hello.' I should explain that she's always been a mite scratchy about the St Andrews connection and particularly of poor Binnie. It's just one of those things. Anyway, the awkward moment passed as soon as the others started hailing Kate and trooping over, and then of course she enjoyed herself very much, though I wished that when she was introducing you to everyone as the author of *Stanley the Suburban Squirrel* she hadn't kept on about it being all based on Prickwell. It's the sort of remark which even if it was true, which it isn't altogether, could lead to all sorts of misunderstandings.

March 10

Full of the joys of spring this morning as I crossed off the last square of my chart, the one framed by red exclamation marks and bells. Rude shock when I telephoned you and Tom answered – 'You're not gone then?' I couldn't help blurting out, but was able to cover the gaffe by adding, 'Oh good, I was afraid I'd missed you both. It's just that—'

'Veronica's gone down to Southampton,' he said. 'She won't be back till this evening. Will you ring again?'

'All right. It was just that *Toys & Games* wanted to interview her. It's not really their scene but as we're so well known in the toys and games world, and in view of the fact that we plan to merchandize Stanley if he catches on, naturally they are—'

'She'll be back this evening.'

'Okay. And how are you?'

'Fine, thanks.'

On which note I thought it best to ring off, though far from reassured. What *is* he up to? I was listening to the news on the radio this morning; some expert or another was confidently forecasting a new Vietcong offensive any day now. If Tom's not careful he'll miss it.

As soon as I come off the M-way I'll try you from a call box. It might be better than waiting till I get home.

Which may be simple enough in books and films but is far from so in the vandals' playground that is Swinging Britain today. Sorry, I'm sounding reactionary. But of the two on the Bath Road one was dead as a doornail and the other missing its works altogether. The one at the station was occupied by two giggling teenage girls who were clearly going to be there for the rest of the night. The one in Boundary Road had its slots stuffed with what seemed to be zinc washers.

Luckily I remembered Bin – friends who live near there, and was able to drop by on some pretext and as soon as was decently possible ask if I might use the phone.

Anyway I was relieved to learn it's nothing to get alarmed about: just a hold-up over visas. I hope I managed to make my inquiry sound properly casual. As for the interview I wanted to arrange, well this is now quite genuine! When I jokingly suggested the idea of some *Stanley* spin-offs to Walter he took it absolutely seriously. 'Good,' he said, 'good thinking.' I've noticed before how some of my best ideas stem from hasty improvisations on quite unrelated matters. The fib is father of the thought!

Not until Saturday now, which means the first chance of a get-together is the day of our little launching party for *Stanley*. This would have been highly appropriate, agreed, except for the small snag that Kate has been invited and will obviously want to be there. She's changed her Meals-on-Wheels duty especially. If she goes to a film or something afterwards she will undoubtedly expect us to go home together, which will ruin everything.

Also, I may be imagining it but . . . well, when you've been married to someone for, er, thirteen years you learn to sense any disaffection. Ever since last weekend she's been . . . not exactly suspicious, but snitchy. When I got home a little later than usual last night, after ringing you and then having to stay for a bit of a chat, she said, 'You're very late tonight.' Yet in the past I've often been home much later to no comment.

It's not as if we gave her any cause for concern during the weekend, either. I mean, you and Tom were very much the affectionate couple and I took good care not to give you any meaningful looks, etcetera, when she was in range. Do you think she'd like a new outfit for the party?

I must say Walter is pushing the boat out. Having a lunchtime function is more expensive for a start, because you have to provide food. But Walter says we should think of our wives for once, it's much easier for them while the children are at school. And apparently the hotel has given us not too unreasonable a quotation for a very nice room with bar and waiters and a cold buffet. I've asked all the literary editors and well-known children's book reviewers.

Of course, Walter insists on having a lot of drears from the toy trade as well. Did that dim girl from *Toys & Games* get you? I suppose it makes sense if *Stanley* does take off, in which case the spin-offs could ultimately be far more profitable for us than the publication. I can just see a nylon fur Stanley with big springy tail and buck teeth and one beady eye closed in a wink. Then there could be Shirley, his mate, with her apron and peg-bag, and Selena, the sexy little neighbour with curling eye-lashes as fancied by Stan, not to mention Mr Bodger the Builder and Councillor Sly, the chairman of the planning committee who takes all his back-handers. The game possibilities are likewise endless.

One thing we must aim for straightaway is to get some of the more suitable stories read on *Jackanory*.

By the way, Walter is being rather stuffy about some of the ideas for the second volume, in particular that very funny one we hatched up over the weekend about the orgy at Councillor Sly's that Stanley and friends break up by dropping fireworks down the chimney. Apart from anything else, he says, it might encourage children to do the same. He also thinks it would be a mistake to have Stanley actually go off to the Treetops Hotel with Selena. He must remain faithful to Shirley.

I keep telling him, we have to aim at a more *knowing* child these days.

March 15

Quick note while washing the car to say that perhaps I was mistaken about the snitchiness. Kate is now looking quite cheerfully ahead to tomorrow. She is very pleased with the little suit we found together in Maidenhead yesterday. What's more, she wants to come up with me in the morning and have her hair done at Sassoon, plus a look at the shops if there's time. Then after the party she will hurry home in time to collect Little Sam from school at three-thirty. I've assured her that she can take the car, I will be perfectly happy to follow later by train!

Chapter Ten

Direct transcript: March 16*

She can't have seen us, honestly. She was too much involved trying to turn right against a No Right Turn sign.

I expect so.

—God, it was rather hairy, though. Just coming up to the lights and there she was in the next lane.

If she'd gone the way I told her she'd have been nowhere near there.

—Perhaps she isn't used to driving in town.

She isn't.

—What is that you're clutching like a charm?

What?

—That thing.

Oh, it's a little tape recorder.

—Does it work?

Of course, listen.

—It's good. What do you use it for, though?

I keep it in the car and, oh, sort of confide to it. I only just remembered to grab it out of the cubbyhole. Would have

* The date has been derived from interior evidence – Ed.

been awkward if Kate had started rummaging round for a paper hankie or something and found it.

—You do like taking chances, don't you?

How do you mean?

—Well, you know, looming all over me even before she'd left. Then us bumping into her when we came out of the lift.

That was Zillah Graves and her abo husband for you. They'd been trying to corner Kate all through the party and patronize her. We spent the whole time dodging them – so they lay in wait in the foyer.

—And finally the bit at the lights. Still that was just hideous luck.

It would have to happen today, of all days.

—Shall we go to the pictures instead?

No!

—Oh God, another bill for moorings. I've only just paid one. Coffee?

Not especially. I mean, unless you want some.

—It's just that it takes the electric blanket twenty minutes to warm up. If I'd known we were coming back I'd have left the convector thingy on. Who was that Gerry somebody it was important to be nice to?

Sorry, what did you say?

—That Gerry someone, at the party.

Oh Gerry Tree. He has a column in the *Standard* about trends and things.

—He said he'd try and do something about Stanley.

I see.

—Well, isn't that good?

Oh yes. Sorry. Very good.

—You're not still brooding?

Of course not.

—You seem very twitchy.

I'm all right.

—Move over then.

Gosh, you're so beautiful.

—I'm sorry, it's too cold to stand around being admired.

You said something about an electric fire last—

—Ow!

What?

—Your feet. Like ice.

Sorry.

—Don't be sorry. Just cuddle me.

Do you think she did see us?

—Kate?

Yes.

—I told you, I don't think so.

She didn't look our way?

—Not that I noticed.

She is always nervous driving in London, and especially in the big car.

—That's what I've been trying to tell you.

What about when she was leaving, and down in the foyer? Was it very obvious?

—I don't know.

You said it was.

—Perhaps it was just me. God, you're not very relaxing.

Supposing she rings the office when she gets home?

—Are all married men like this?

I'm sorry.

—Don't *be* sorry!

If maybe I phoned her, as soon as she's picked up Little Sam from school . . . would you mind?

—Help yourself.

In a quarter of an hour, say.

—Are you sure you wouldn't rather sprint home with the message personally?

*

135

It's all right. I got her, said I just wanted to make sure she'd managed the Three-Litre in London all right. She was fine, enjoyed the party she said, never even mentioned you.

—Great.

Gosh, now I love you. You're delicious. What are you?

—What do you mean?

You're supposed to say 'delicious' back to me. It's an army thing. You know, you idle man you! What are you? An idle man, sarge. You are golden and fragrant and gorgeous. What are you?

—Sleepy.

I kiss one eye . . . other eye . . . ear-lobe . . . other ear . . . nose . . . other nose . . .

—I've only got one nose.

Sssh. No one need ever know.

—First you were all doomy, now you're rabitting on—

Not rabbiting. Squirrelling. I am Stanley the Suburban Squirrel, with my bushy tail and my bright little eye and I'm coming scamper-scamper-scamper up the smooth branch of the beautiful smooth tree—

—You're tickling me—

To where the sweetest hazel nuts cluster. Yum yum yum.

—Mmm.

Then I do dee-dee-dee-dee-dee down the slippery trunk.

—Oh God, what now?

And with one bound Stan leaps free! And he's flying, flapping, falling . . . through . . . the . . . sky . . . yum.

—Mmmmm.

—Oh God, was I asleep?

Like a child.

—What are you looking for?

Nothing. What are all these little bottles?

—Pills.

136

What sort of pills?

—The usual assortment. Nothing fancy.

You shouldn't need all that rubbish.

—That's what Tom says. He uses worse. Hey, you didn't have that nasty little thing going after all, did you?

Now would I? I was just going to record something while I remembered it.

—Remembered what?

It doesn't matter. I'll interview you instead, Miss Hart, would you say that Stanley acquitted himself reasonably well on that occasion.

—Mmmm.

You're supposed to say 'Definitely' or even 'Definitely, yes.'

—Why?

Because people always do.

—What time is it?

Half-past five.

—I love it when it starts to get dark and there's that sort of dove-coloured sky through the skylight – see – and you can hear the traffic on the Embankment and the tide sploshing about underneath.

That's not what you can hear now because, you see, I crept out and cut the ropes and we've drifted away down the river and out to sea and we won't see land again until we get to Tierra del Fuego.

—Where?

Margate, then.

—I pretend that, too, sometimes. It's good for getting to sleep. I shut my eyes and count the bridges as we leave them behind one by one, only I can never remember the right order and get in a muddle. And sometimes I make it that the boat is sinking, it's getting heavier and heavier and slower and slower and the water is closing over the top—

You mustn't, not even in a pretend—

—And it's so quiet. You sleep and sleep and sleep—
Veronica, no!
—It's all right. It's only when I'm lonely sometimes. I can
feel your heart beating.
I can feel yours.

—What do you want?
My socks. Where's the light switch?
—I'll do it. What time is it now?
Nearly seven.
—Do you have to go?
Do I! I'm going to be so late already, by the time I get to
Paddington. Even if there's a train straightaway.
—Take my car if you like.
Where would I leave it . . ?
—No, take it all the way home, I meant.
Honestly? Are you sure?
—If it makes life easier.
It transforms it! I'll take good care of the car. I've often
driven Kate's. Bring it back in the morning first thing?
—Whatever suits you.
You're a poppet!
—Thanks.
Well . . . see you in the morning.
—Aren't you going to kiss me?
Oh yes.
—Graham.
Mm?
—What are you going to tell Kate.
I don't need to tell her anything now, do I?
—Ah, silly of me. Don't forget your toy.
Gosh, nearly did.

Chapter Eleven

March 17 (morning)

It all worked out ridiculously easily. I had driven Kate's little bus often enough to have the hang of the double-declutching and, you know, the rather absent-minded response of the little motor that burbles away behind you. It seemed only five minutes up to the North End Road and at that time of evening scarcely another five to the flyover. Never mind that on the motorway, against the wind, it was a job to hold fifty. I felt – well, not exactly relaxed, though obviously it was a great relief to be so miraculously delivered from the certainty of creeping home late and guilty. It was . . . it was almost as if I were disembodied. I could put myself back in your boat, in your bed. I could hear your voice still, smell your skin and your hair and the sheets. I could put myself ahead, to being home again and talking to Kate, even what I would say to her and the mood I'd be in. But the me that drove the little Fiat along between these two realities was just a sort of automatic pilot, without feelings.

What a load of nonsense! I expect it was no more than the unfamiliarity of the vehicle on top of an action-packed day!

At all events, the automatic pilot guided us unerringly to Prickwell Station carpark. That was another funny thing, I have to admit I don't remember working out any conscious plan but of course it was the only possible place: the station was where I would logically arrive; the carpark was where I could safely leave the car and safely retrieve same today. All that remained to be done was ring Kate and ask her to pick me up.

'Oh dear,' she said as she saw me. 'Did it go on all afternoon?'

'Did what go on?' I said, startled.

'The party, of course. Two hours was more than enough for me.'

I suppose I did look a bit washed out, especially in the ghastly yellow streetlights of Station Approach. And that, apart from a desultory post-mortem over the supper table, was all. The chatter and the cigarette smoke, rather than the drink – of which she rarely takes more than a glass – had left poor Kate with a slight head, so we both went to bed early.

In the middle of the night I awoke and thought at first I been dreaming. Then I gave myself a slight turn by remembering I'd left this little gadget in a car whose sun roof Kate's insurance company regards as an open invitation to the light-fingered. What's more, the most recent 'take' was – well, as I'm sure you guessed, I was trying to record actual conversation during the course of the day. It was partly in the nature of an experiment, partly because . . . oh, it doesn't matter. I haven't played it back. Perhaps I never will.

Anyway, the fact that I am chuntering on to it now makes it unnecessary for me to add that the machine was still there this morning amid the jolly litter of your glove compartment.

Indeed the whole operation has continued smoothly. It was the work of but a minute to park my own car at the station and collect yours, even if the attendant did gape at me, silly old fool. That strange disembodied feeling of last

140

night has faded. To think that I shall see you again very soon, however unromantic the hour, gives my heart a jolt of excitement. Speed, little Fiat, speed! By the way, I put two gallons in your tank.

March 17 (evening)

How you happened to be occupied at the precise moment I arrived was a bonus. I tip-toed across the bridge of decks. The sun glinted on the river and the aroma of coffee wafted from someone's galley – or was it yours? Even as I tapped lightly on the bulkhead I heard the faint hiss of water.

'Who is it?' you called as I stepped down inside.

'Your car, madam.'

Under a frilly plastic cap, big misty eyes peered short-sightedly round the edge of the sliding door into your little bathroom. 'Oh, it's you,' you said. 'I'm in the shower.'

'All mod con.'

'The same bit of water goes round and round or something, but it's all right if you don't wash your hair at the same time.'

'Can I come in?'

'God, there's not room for one, let alone two.'

'No, just to say hallo.'

'Same applies. I'll be out in a sec. There's some coffee on the stove.'

My heart was thumping all over again as I poured a cup. I couldn't think of anything to say, so I called, 'I put two gallons in.'

'What?'

'I put two gallons in. Your car.'

'Oh, thanks.'

I heard the hiss of water cease and all at once there you were, dripping and unselfconscious. If I stared, I'm sorry. The thing is, you forget how unflawed and marvellous is

141

the body of a young woman. It is with . . . it is not that . . .
Kate is still most attractive, without any doubt. I was thinking actually of another girl, the one on that picnic I tried to
tell you of once. In the cold light of day, all goose pimples
and you know, sagging, it was just NOT sexy; the very
opposite. I mean, things were never quite the same again
there.

You were taking some stuff to one of your magazines, so
after you had dressed and swallowed a cup of coffee and
attempted to tidy up a little, you took me the rest of the way
into town. It gave me a warm, domestic feeling, going to
work together like any little loving couple. At the same time
each spin of the wheels brought us nearer the moment of
parting.

'It buzzes along, your little car,' I said. 'You must have
had a new elastic band recently.'

'What's that?' you said.

'Nothing. A joke we have with the kids.'

'You're dotty about your children, aren't you?'

'Am I? Well, they're my livelihood, in a sense – or knowing what they like is.'

Actually, I hadn't thought of it that way before.

All too soon I stood on the pavement and watched you
weave away into the traffic. And now I can think of nothing
else, I only long to see you again. Like an X-ray plate that
tells its story only when it's developed, the truth stares me
in the face at last: I'm in love.

March 18

'For the tiny sophisticates of Hampstead, Highgate,
Wimbledon Common and other leafy suburbs, stories of
our little furry friends will never be quite the same again.
Nor, for that matter, will the furry friends themselves if
they happen to be – as they probably are – common grey

142

squirrels. For author-illustrator Veronica Hart and a new children's publisher, Hale Godley, have exposed the secret life of S. Squirrel, Esq., in *Stanley the Suburban Squirrel*, out this week.

'Stan, it seems, is sly, scheming and sexy. He conducts a running guerilla campaign against Bodger the Builder, the developer whose advancing tide of houses is destroying the squirrels' habitat. He teases the vicar and other worthies. He delights in making mischief – and capital – out of furtive little goings-on among the two-legged locals, unperturbed by the reflection that his own morals leave something to be desired.

'The ambience is so authentic that it comes as a slight surprise to learn that Veronica Hart lives on a houseboat near far-from-leafy Lots Road power station. A slim, pretty 24-year-old who looks at the world guardedly from behind fashionably owlish glasses, she admits however to having done some field work. Neither Wimbledon nor Highgate Woods was the model for Stanley's suburb, but a much farther-flung, more properly exurbanite, community: Prickwell, on the Berks–Bucks border.'

You must have seen the *Standard* by now, even if you hadn't when I caught you on the phone at last. If still not, I have three copies with me, as well as the bottle of champagne. A celebration is certainly called for. Walter is cock-a-hoop and says it is just the kind of item which other papers will follow up, especially London editors of provincial journals. Be with you in a few minutes.

March 19

Later home last night than I should have been without some good reason for being late. A distinct snitchiness was evident. With the aid of the *Standard* and the news of other coups to come I did my best to babble convincingly of

143

business, and thanks to your little effort this morning I am sure everything is now okay.

All the while, of course, I wanted only to remember the warmth of the electric fire, the cold taste of the champagne, the intensity with which you read Gerry Tree's piece, the avidity of your kisses, the telephone trilling as another journalist tracked you down and then the *Today* programme to arrange this morning's interview.

We all listened at the breakfast table, though I had to shush Little Sam more than once. 'Is that *really* the lady what came here?' he said incredulously.

'The lady *that* came here,' I tried to correct him for the millionth time.

'Veruca,' said Janet, to tease her sister.

'Where's thingy?' said Miranda, ignoring her.

'Tom,' said Janet.

'He was going to the Far East, wasn't he?' said Kate, a little pointedly, perhaps. 'Would he be back yet?'

'I've no idea,' I said. 'I should think so, though.'

Then you mentioned her – Kate, that is, as the person who had the original idea. Nobody was expecting it. Kate went positively pink, the children were wide-eyed with surprise, Miranda clapped her hands in glee. I must say it was brilliantly tactful, and generous on your part. And tomorrow, television! They tell me I can watch in the hospitality room, as they call it, and afterwards I'll run you home if you don't have your car. But I mustn't be too late, honestly.

Off-air recording. March 20

—You don't agree then, Miss Hart, that Stanley is a subversive influence among the nursery school set?

—God, no.

Nor a sort of *Peyton Place* for toddlers?

—You know, it's just a furry animal story, up-dated a bit.

And not – I quote from the *Sun* this morning, – a 'sizzling social satire for the seven-year old'?

—Definitely not, no.

So you're quite unrepentant?

—Right.

Thank you Miss Hart.

And now at the London Zoo a very different—

Remembered to take the little recorder in with me but in the excitement, dammit, omitted to switch on until the last few seconds. Never mind, you were awfully good. They were a funny lot in the hospitality room – you know, the wife of the man who bit the heads off rats, the husband of the woman who was getting up that petition, a whole crowd who'd come along with the folk group, but they were all very attentive during your bit. 'Good on her,' the old ploughman said, the one who'd been on first. 'She doan't give that booy any change, do she?' Actually he lives in Leytonstone, he told me, which didn't quite accord with the rural image they were trying to conjure up.

And now it is after nine and I'm still on the motorway, and though the television thing is a watertight business excuse, there may well be a little sniffiness in store. I know it's difficult with all the different jobs you are up to, but if you could remember to keep the odd afternoon clear it would be a help. Then after Easter, as I told you, all being well, keep fingers crossed, with any luck, Kate's thinking of taking the children up to their granny's in Huntingdonshire and will stay at least one night herself. Fasten your seat-belt then!

Of course I didn't want to leave you, what with Easter coming up and four days exile from London, not to mention a threat to next week's all-night date. But we had been together half the afternoon; it was a chance to get home a little less late than I have been managing lately. And as you'll see in a moment, just as well I did! I was threading my way up to the Cromwell Road, all set to record some golden moments while they were still newly minted when suddenly I saw Brigadier Max – remember him? It was near Empress House where he commands a typewriter. He was standing right on the edge of the pavement, as if looking for a taxi, and obviously would spot me.

I pulled up and he hopped in, pleased to have a lift all the way home though curiously unimpressed – I thought – by the accident that I should be passing. 'Was about to give you up,' he said mysteriously.

Apparently Sue Kennerly had rushed up to town and taken his car off to Essex or East Anglia or wherever the daughter is at university. The baby is threatening to arrive ahead of schedule and Mama wants to be there to help, whether the kids like it or not.

Naturally I was full of Stanley's doings, in which context I couldn't resist talking about you. It gave me an absurd little thrill, just like a schoolboy casually mentioning the name of his secret sweetheart. Max was very warm in his interest, I will say that for him; of course he had met you. He told me wryly of his own progress in finding a job when he retires in the autumn. The firmest proposal he's had yet is to be bursar of some fiddling little adult education college in the Midlands. Can you imagine? Ordering the lavatory paper and so on! What a job for a man in his prime.

I know you found him very boring, and of course his career has been entirely of his own choosing, and at our expense to boot; nevertheless I couldn't help feeling acutely aware of the difference between the 'high' on which I am riding these days – or was until today – and the trough in which he must find himself. Not even the ceremonial farewell parade a regimental soldier would have, I daresay; just clear out his desk and creep away – to another desk.

I asked him in for a drink, feeling very virtuous in the possession of such an excellent alibi, only to find Kate already expecting him for supper. As I should have guessed, she had been involved in getting Sue Kennerly off, taking her to the station, etcetera, and she had been trying to phone me at the office later to ask me to pick up Max. By dint of some fast thinking and flannelling on about conflicting messages, I managed to convey the impression that I had indeed gone looking for him, and it was entirely due to a muddle at his end that we were late. But I shudder to think of the pitfalls that yawned on every side.

After Max had gone home to bed, Kate was very subdued. I wondered if perhaps she was depressed at the prospect of losing Max and Sue as neighbours – she has always got on much better with them than I have. I tried to be as sympathetic and understanding as possible, but when I asked if she'd thought any more about taking the children up to her mother's she snapped, 'I'm not sure if I can go now.' Also, if I am going to have to ferry Max to and fro again tomorrow that is going to ruin another day.

March 26

All is well. It's not what I suspected she suspected at all! It is Binnie Davies she was worrying about, the girl we were talking to in the local pub that time – the one who came over first, with the auburn hair you thought was perhaps touched up and the rather whoopee figure. For some reason Kate has never taken to her. It's partly the university

147

thing I told you of, partly – well, no smoke without fire: I won't deny we had a pretty torrid little scene going in the not too dim and distant past. But it's water under the bridge now, especially as her bloody mother is back for the Easter holidays.

It all came out last night. I haven't mentioned it before because it's simply not worth mentioning, but the last time I saw the lady she was full of some crack-pot scheme her no-good husband was contemplating. The idea was to throw in a perfectly good, if dreary, job at the local firm and become an agent for some range of cosmetics I've never heard of. Apparently you are given – or rather, pay good money for – a franchise and then appoint sub-agents who in turn pay you. Hmmm. Well, she rang up the other evening to say he'd taken the plunge and she was going to help him and would we like to flog scent and shampoo and bubble baths to our friends? Can you imagine! I didn't even bother to call Kate to the phone. As I said to her afterwards, 'How can they bring themselves to approach people they *know*?'

I suppose we were chatting for five or ten minutes, exchanging a bit of gossip and – on my part – listening to a few moans about the unions and the workers. She assumes everyone is a Tory. And Binnie being Binnie there was the inevitable request for a favour, in this case concerning her car, on which she now relies even more, etcetera. We have this very good mechanic who services our cars, especially Kate's little bus, being Italian. You can't understand a frocking word he says, to use his own commonest adjective, but he has magic fingers with a Fiat 500. Ever since I ushered Binnie along with hers – she's got one, too – she seems to expect me to act as go-between.

Anyway, as I said before it can't have been more than ten minutes and all conducted perfectly openly. But Kate said quite sharply, 'I must say you were being very affable,' and

'What were you fixing up?' 'Nothing,' I exploded. It was too boring to have to start explaining the Dino business at this stage.

Then yesterday it seems that she had been dusting my little den and found the telephone index open at letter 'D'. As if I would need to look up a number that I used to know as well as I now know yours! In fact I had been looking up the aforesaid Dino. Of course I pretended that it was on her behalf. 'You said something about a funny noise in second.'

'I said next time it's due for service would do.'

'It's best never to leave these things. Honestly, I go out of my way to look after things like that for you, and all I get for my pains are dark suspicions.'

She gave me a searching look from those big searching eyes. 'There's nothing going on?'

'Of course there isn't.'

'Truth?'

'You know me. I'm no good at fibs.'

The outcome of which absurd misunderstandings is – wait for it! – that she is going to buzz up to Huntingdonshire with the children after all, though she talks of returning the next day herself, there are so many good works to be done. I told her she needs a little break and should stay a week. Whatever she decides we shall have one night together.

By the way, it's a little boy: the Kennerly girl's baby. Six pounds odd, and perfectly lusty. Max brought the news this morning. He's going there by train this evening, which means I also don't need to worry about giving him a lift home. See you!

Chapter Twelve

March 31

Now don't worry, whatever happens you won't be personally at risk unless we're all absolutely bankrupted by it, which is just too fantastic to contemplate. But the fact is there has been a lawyer's letter from Smailes, the wretched Prickwell jerry-builder, claiming that he has been held up to ridicule and contempt by *Stanley the Suburban Squirrel*. Walter is being jolly sensible and unflustered. He has a Q.C. friend who thinks it would be very difficult to prove anything should it come to law. On the other hand there have been these silly insinuations in the Press that it's all based on Prickwell and therefore by inference Mr Bodger equals Mr Smailes – unfortunately the local rags did not fail to pick up this juicy suggestion. I'm afraid some blame also attaches to Kate, who would keep bragging in similar vein.

What concerns me most at the moment is that nothing should be allowed to blight our night together tomorrow. You'll have to know about the boring business, if you don't already: After all, you're involved. But I'll take good care to treat it rather more fliply than I did just now. That has always been one of the objects of this exercise, to compose the right attitude, etcetera. The attitude just now is that

150

even libel suits shrink into insignificance when I think of you, which is about ninety-five per cent of waking time plus a more than fair share of dream time. In church on Sunday I suffered the exact reverse of the spiritual experience you're supposed to have in church. I was filled with disbelief. I looked at prissy young Father Thingy in his white and gold, at the congregation ploughing through gloomy hymns, at the masses of flowers which Kate had helped to arrange and the waxy, lifeless Easter lilies which she says cost some absurd sum of money that might be better employed to feed the poor. I looked at her and at the kids fidgeting and whispering between us, and felt that I only had to blink for it all to vanish and never bother me again.

It may be that the absence of the Kennerlys from their accustomed place by our side heightened the sense of isolation. The boys are on some school camp, Sue is still in Essex, Max came back but all weekend was being summoned to various mysterious conferences in Whitehall, and is now staying at his club. When I asked Kate what it was all about she snapped 'How should I know?' If they go, in a funny way it will be the end for us.

Erase, erase.

Where shall it be, our night together? Your boat is full of romantic associations for me. We could lie together and listen to the sounds of the river and the sleeping city.

Our house on the heath might be more romantic for you, with the smoky, misty night smell and the birds in the morning. For once it will be free of neighbourly observation. I have already suggested Mrs Wild comes in the afternoon instead of the morning so that she can give the dog his dinner and a run – and not come cycling up at 9 a.m. to find you in a lacy peignoir!

But I leave it to you. One small factor is that I shan't have any transport. With the children to take plus enough changes of clothes and toys to last a siege, Kate will obviously need the big car. And as a consequence of that silly misunderstanding over the telephone index I seem to have committed myself to putting her little Fiat into Dino's for a check-up.

Later

Okay: aboard the good ship Venus, then! I can easily come up by train. And next morning, as far as the office is concerned, I shall be doing a spot of battery re-charging.

April 1

The toilet of the 9.07 to Town may not be the choicest place in which these thoughts have been committed but I must put down, and then try to forget, immediate reactions to a chance encounter which you would refuse to accept in a novel. Duly left Kate's little car at Dino's with just enough time to walk on to the station, which I preferred to do because he was already protesting about something in his incoherent way, with much gesticulation and frocking and blinding, and I couldn't face five minutes more of it at close range.

As I reached the station a fat beige Jaguar swished into the car park. I recognized it straightaway, likewise the thick-necked figure crouched over the wheel. It was Smailes! Presumably he was after the 9.07 too. Guessing – wrongly, as things turned out – that with all his ill-gotten wealth he would travel First Class, and was sure to be a smoker, I lurked behind my *Guardian* by the six-car stop with a view to boarding a second-class non-smoker in the leading coach.

Unfortunately it was only a three-car train – God knows, they're crowded enough already. I had to join an undignified scramble back down the platform and get in where I could. To my embarrassment I found myself standing right over Smailes, who needless to say had grabbed a seat and was deep in conversation with some crony. What's more I was trapped between other standees and couldn't move down the coach.

'If they think they can get away with this they can think again,' Smailes was saying. 'They'll pay for it, all right, or my name's not Ted Smailes. All that laughing behind the backs of their 'ands, so bloody superior they think they are. I know who it is, don't worry – and the wife with all her airs. Tried to muck me up when we was doing Nuthatch Gardens, with a petition and all that rubbish. Waste o' time. Just held me up six months, that's all, which didn't matter because by the time I was selling the price was up five hundred each 'ouse. And all the while they were trying to build in their own back yard. Sold the plot before they moved theirselves, they did. By Christ, I'm going to cane that pair.'

At which point I thought advisable to start excusing myself towards the toilet, lest he should look up from his narrative. No doubt he had just heard from those lawyers in London about Walter's reply and was on his way to see them. I'm told they are specialists in screwing damages out of innocent victims of our absurd libel laws. Well, we shall see. The important thing is not to let the ill luck of running into Smailes cast a gloom over tonight. I feel I've got it off my chest a little already. If I tell Walter as well, making it a bit of a joke, it should fall into perspective.

By the way, Max Kennerly is going to Northern Ireland. That's what all the coming and going was leading up to. Apparently the man who was going to do this particular job was in a helicopter crash – do you remember it in the papers? Max was rather cut up because he knew him. Now he's taking on the job himself, though, he's like a dog with

153

two tails, according to Kate; I haven't seen him yet. It is hardly the kind of soldiering I would fancy if I were in the army, which God forbid – skulking around behind vizors and shields and gunning down civilians. But, if it's your profession I suppose you don't worry about things like that. The main thing is that it puts off his retirement for a couple of years at least. The college post in the Midlands is quite forgotten.

I thought I heard him playing that plonking music when I got home last night but as I said, they're away. It must have been the radio, unless Kate has the record.

Till tonight!

April 2, a.m.

I, Graham Lewis Godley, being of sound mind and not too decrepit body, I hope you will agree, do solemnly affirm my love for you, Anna Veronica Hart, spinster of this parish, and furthermore testify that you have the most adorable and delicious and rounded little—

—What are you on about now?

Committing myself.

—In the middle of the night, do you have to?

It's important. You should listen. Anyway, it's six in the morning.

—That *is* the middle of the night. Come back to sleep.

All right, then, I whisper. Beside me your hair is a dark tangle on the blur of the pillow, though I know it to be fair and glossy. I see the curve of your cheek and your little nose. When you buried your face in the pillow to exclude the day it sort of squashed like a little girl's. Beneath the sheets I feel your leg pressed against mine. In your sleep your foot twitched several times. Your hand – your right hand – lies in my left. I see also the thick yellowy brown

154

curtains over the porthole and out of the corner of my eye the varnished wood ceiling.

Have we drifted under the bridges and out to sea this time? No, I hear the same old creaks from the other boats and the ropes that join them. A barge went by a little while ago that I felt rather than heard.

What you were saying before we slept excites and frightens and perplexes me. I had always assumed that you and Tom were – well, a couple. That he lived here and would sooner or later return here, preferably later. Now you think he has been back in London and may even have gone off again without seeing you. Some things he left here in the boat have vanished and the old queer who lives on *Esmeralda IV* said he'd seen a red sports car parked in the yard, which would be his (Tom's) ex-wife's, formerly his. When you rang her she was very cagey, and when you rang again an answering machine said something about her being in New York. In any case there are other birds, including one who is Lady Somebody and rich.

It is a world I read about but do not know.

Then you cried and clung to me and said, 'Oh God, I only want someone to be with, someone to wake up with.'

A young girl in need of care and affection.

But love, too; you speak often of love. 'I was in love then,' or 'I was in love you see,' as if that explained everything. And a funny, troubling thing you said when telling of how Tom left his wife for you, you thought, and it was plain to you this was the height, the Everest, of love. If you're waiting for the same gesture from me it, well, for a start it won't be a gesture, it will be real and awful and marvellous and for ever.

If I were to do it at all I would have to do it now.
—Do what?

You are awake, then? I was saying . . . oh nothing. It doesn't matter.

—Go on; something about you'd have to do it now.

Get up, that's all. If I don't I'll stay here for ever.

—Why not?

I meant it seriously.

—So did I.

For me to move in?

—If you want to. But you won't.

How do you know?

—You're too married.

More so than Tom was?

—God, yes.

I might surprise you.

—Leave Kate? The children, your home, your—

Oh my God!

—You see.

Oh hell, the poor little brute.

—*Who?*

Rastus.

—Rastus?

The dog. Our dog. He's been shut up in the house since yesterday. I've been thinking Mrs Wild would give him a run but I've just remembered, I put her off. She's looking in this afternoon instead.

—Won't that do?

No! Poor thing, he'll be bursting.

—Where are you going?

I'll come straight back.

—Can't you ring her?

Not on the phone.

—Neighbours?

I told you, away. Can I borrow your car again?

—I'll need it later.

I'll come straight back. Stay there.

—I'm coming with you.

Like that?

—I'll wrap myself in the rug. Then you can carry me into your house like Cleopatra.

Better not.

—Why?

Just in case. I'll be back by nine, honestly. We'll have breakfast. Wait for me.

—Whatever you say.

You will, won't you? – wait for me? Be here?

He was all right, the silly old sausage. No signs of distress, could hardly be bothered to wag his tail. I took him the speediest circuit ever of the beech clump, pond and back by Max's gravel drive where he likes to sniff. The phone was ringing as we returned. It was Kate. 'You're bright and early,' I said.

'Tried last night, no reply.'

'Must have been taking Rastus for his run.'

Was I in for a cross-examination? But no. All she wanted was to say she had this notion to come back via Colchester and call in to gush all over the Kennerly baby and take a Babygro or something from us. The only thing is that this would mean she'd be home much later.

'Of course, of course. Take your time,' I assured her. 'I can manage. Why not come back tomorrow?'

I thought she was going to agree but she said no, she'd be home tonight. Never mind, we've got all day. Oh why didn't I let you come wrapped in a rug? Speed little Fiat, speed!

April 2, p.m.

At which point things started to go horribly wrong. I've been too strung up to set anything down so far. I admit I had been pushing your little bus pretty hard along the

157

motorway out, but they're built to survive a nation of maniac drivers. It was probably when I'd come off the M-way, the long hill up to Boundary Road, that the damage was done. It's deceptive, you don't notice the gradient and I was trying to get past a stupid great ten-tonner – indeed I had to get past, because the idiot behind me had also moved out to overtake and was sitting right on my tail, flashing his lights. So down into third and foot right down. Just made it before the crossroads. The engine note was a bit hair-raising, but the trouble with this kind of Nemesis is that it always takes a few minutes to brew to perfection and I was on to the motorway before a nasty little noise, tinny and popping at the same time if you can imagine that, was insistent enough to banish hope it might go away. By then the smell of burning oil was also wafting in, followed by actual blue smoke and a warning blink from a rare performer among the warning lights plus a definite impression, whether psychosomatic or real, that everything was about to lock solid. I pulled off at the next exit, which luckily is only three miles farther along – only! It seemed like three hundred, with a groan every mile – and hobbled back along the Bath Road. It happened to Kate once: a blown rocker-box gasket, and though it is not the end of the world it seemed like it then: a paradox, in fact, since it was to the World's End I was burning to get.

Dino was just opening up his yard, thank goodness. I saw a ray of hope. If Kate's car were ready I could be on my way again within five minutes. Even if it weren't – well, it was only in for a service and check-up. I drove your ailing, fuming baby right up to his den and turned on the act that is part of doing business with Dino. You gibber and roll your eyes and point to your watch, and generally pretend you're an imbecile who couldn't keep a wheelbarrow on the road without his forbearance. 'Gasket finito,' I shouted, 'like Signora's that time. Can you fix dam' quick?'

158

'No, no, no do,' he said as he always says. 'Ecco, I got seven frocking cars waiting already—'

'For me, Dino'.

All the while he'd been peering into the works and shaking his head and sighing. 'Tomorrow, maybe.'

'Not domani. Tonight, eh?'

'No do, no do.'

'All right, domani, but domani first thing, eh? Where is Signora's little auto by the way – my signora's?'

'No feenish yet. Tomorrow she wanted, you tell me—'

'Can't help that. Just point me to it.'

At which point his telephone jangled and I left him conducting another of his totally incomprehensible transactions. Kate's little car was where I'd left it twenty-four hours before, next to a mouldering old Buick in which Dino's hens roost when they're not occupying anyone else's vehicle. I doubt if he'd touched it. But just to be on the way again was an enormous boost to morale. I drove reasonably steadily and almost felt relaxed enough to say a few words to this gadget, though as I filtered down through Fulham I don't mind saying my heart was beating. I just couldn't believe it when the fellow in the little office called, 'I think she's gone out, Guv.'

You hadn't even locked the door. Inside it was like the *Mary Celeste*: the bed-clothes flung aside, your last night's dress where you had draped it over the back of a chair, my loose change where I had left it on the locker, along with your pills and litter of bracelets and ear-rings and elastic bands and pens and pencils and sticks of that red chalk stuff you like to use and an old dried-up apple core that must have been there at least three weeks. But no glasses – you'd taken your glasses. The damp towel on the little bathroom floor was probably from last night. Hard to sort out the muddle in the little kitchen. It didn't look as if you had stopped for any breakfast, though.

I stayed for five or ten minutes, hoping against hope you had only gone in search of bread or milk or something. Then – honestly I wasn't meaning to pry, just vaguely trying to tidy up, and there was this sheaf of sketches on thick grey paper under the cushions of the long seat: all of Tom, and very good, only some of them when he's got nothing on and is muscular and hairy and twenty-eight.

Suddenly, I had to move on. But where? I scribbled that note for you and left it with the car keys and started walking. Got a taxi in the Kings Road and went to the office, of course – well, it was somewhere you would try sooner or later if you were looking for me.

The news there was fully in keeping with the day: Smailes's crook solicitors are unimpressed by Walter's reply and say their client will press for satisfaction. And for extra cheer, there is a fresh Mugwumps crisis looming; not entirely Zillah Graves' and hubby's doing this time; the fact is that they have had an offer of a takeover, the whole Mugwump industry to be bought up by this Australian corporation. It will give them the capital they're always bemoaning the lack of, but where it leaves us is not yet clear. Nowhere, if I know that gamey couple.

Only when Mrs Cernik had dropped several arch remarks did I realize I hadn't shaved. Luckily Walter, being black around the jowls, keeps a Remington in our wash-room.

The hours passed in a sort of numbness. Whenever Mrs Cernik was sufficiently occupied not to be watching me, I dialled your number and heard it ringing, ringing. Once I got the engaged tone, and feverishly re-dialled over and over again until once more it rang unanswered. Someone else must have been trying.

Walter and I went for a mournful drink at the end of the day. 'There's always the Ulster game,' he said. 'How are you getting on with it?'

Not very fast, I had to tell him. But at least I can ask Max for some first-hand advice if he comes home on leave. On the train it suddenly hit me that you might have assumed I had stayed at home and were trying to get me there. Was filled with impatience lest (*a*) this was so and (*b*) Kate should get there before me. Treated myself to Harry Holden's taxi, though the villain charges the best part of a quid to the heath.

The house was empty and cold. I kicked Rastus out to take himself for a walk: it was all his fault, stupid animal.

Out of the blue the phone gave that little shiver that means it is going to ring. It rang! The peep-peep-peep of an STD call box gave way to a girlish voice saying diffidently, 'Oh, you're there—'

'Where are you?' I screamed, but even as I screamed I knew it wasn't you, it was Kate.

Surprised, she said, 'With Sue and Sarah and – and the baby and everyone. It's a dear little baby.'

'Is it?' Such encounters usually result in her being broody for the next seven days.

'The only thing is that I got lost and couldn't find the place and now it's so late I thought I might come on in the morning . . .'

'That's all right.'

'Are you sure you can manage?'

'Of course I can manage.'

I rode Janet's bike to Dino's yard, my knees banging against the handlebars. Your little Fiat had been left out, and glory be, the keys were lodged on the sun flap, which is where he puts them if you want to collect out of hours. So once more, as the high yellow lights come on, the three lanes of Madam Four lure me to London at a dizzy fifty miles an hour. If you're still not there I'll get something to eat and try again. I'll find you somehow. I must find you. Until I've found you I can't think, I can't decide.

Chapter Thirteen

April 3

The boat was just as I had left it – or rather, as she had left it: same litter, same unmade bed, same crocks, the keys and the note where I had left them. I felt tired and hungry and drove up to the Provençal for a steak and half a carafe which in a dull, greedy way I enjoyed.

She arrived back about ten. I heard a car door slam, then the tap of high heels on the deck. She was wearing what looked like an expensive if somewhat creased outfit of which I only exactly remember the colour, which was an opaque green like marzipan. Her face was pale with shadows under the eyes.

'Oh God, you haven't been here all day?'

'No. I brought your car back.'

'I saw it. And another next to it. I thought I was seeing double.'

'It's a long story. It doesn't matter.'

'I'm sorry about this morning. It was just – oh, the dog and everything. And then you didn't come back—'

'Things went wrong.'

'I expect you want to know where I've been.'

'I was rather wondering.'

'Paris, actually. Clive's got his own aeroplane, you see.'

'Ah, Clive.'

'Did I tell you about Clive? He's very rich and busy and everything. He sweeps up and sweeps you off, you know.'

That was the gist of it, anyway, likewise an indication of the funny flat way we conversed, like characters in a play.

'You're not cross?' she asked eventually. She was shivering slightly, from cold and tiredness and also, I now see, from fear that I was going to make a scene. Once or twice she had said things about people being cross with her, as if this was what she dreaded most in life, next to being alone.

If I had gone out to her then she would have burst into tears, and where would it have ended? Instead I just said, 'No, I'm not cross,' in a non-committal, boring voice.

She yawned. 'God, I'm tired. Thanks for tidying up, you needn't.'

'It passed the time.'

She went into the little loo and called through the door, 'Were you thinking of staying, by the way?'

'If I may.'

'Well, I wouldn't let Clive and I'm exhausted and I've got a bit of cystitis and I *must* get some sleep. I've got a job to finish tomorrow.'

'I'll take the sofa.'

Around five a.m. I woke up for the sixth or seventh and final time. Gloomy thoughts were waiting patiently for me. Things were no clearer, just drearier. Smailes's libel suit loomed huge and threatening. At the half hour I made a cup of tea. At six o'clock I pulled on the remainder of my clothes and scooped up change and keys and oddments and found myself well and truly in this godawful muddle. I seemed to have both sets of Fiat keys. I stared at them stupidly wondering which was the one I wanted: the ring with the little moulting, mangey spider or the one with the St Christopher medallion. I had a clear mental picture of

163

both charms swinging below the steering column within the last twenty-four hours, but which came first? Both could be Veronica-type possessions, neither seemed very Kateish, though key-rings were favourite birthday and Christmas presents from the children, along with ball-points and little bottles of bubble-bath. There had been a little furry creature once, was it a spider?

The simple way out of the quandary was to see which key fitted Kate's car. I crept out and trod as delicately as possible across the bridge of decks. It was – is – a nice morning. The sun sparkled on the river. The two little blue Fiats looked very cute, parked nose to tail. Kate's would be the one in front, or had I backed Veronica's in ahead of Kate's when I came back from the restaurant? The more I thought about it the less sure I became.

I studied the number plates. Should have known Kate's but never had bothered to memorize it. Wait a minute – the children had a joke about an *ugh* sound in the letters. The one in front was UJH, the one behind UGL.

There was nothing for it but to wake the sleeping beauty. I don't know which pills she had been taking but it took some time. I dangled the two sets of keys above her and said, 'Which is yours?'

'What are you talking about? What time is it?'

I remembered her glasses, and found them and steered them on to her nose. She had drifted off again. I shook her. She reluctantly focused. I said very carefully, 'Which key-ring and keys are yours?'

No answer, so I shook her and said it again.

She woke up and said clearly and plaintively, 'Neither. I've never seen them before. Mine's got a rude thing on that Tom brought back from America once, two lovers twined together only round the wrong way.'

In the light of which it didn't matter much which I took. I

settled for St Christopher and UJH. And now I head once more along the pitiless motorway. Siemens, Turriff and Heston Services have trudged by. Next, the Feltham exit to look forward to, then whoopee – London Airport.

If the car is not Veronica's it is either Kate's or someone else's altogether. And that someone else must be – right first time: Binnie Davies. She caused that row with Kate not a million years ago, indeed only last week, when she rang to ask me to arrange an overhaul with Dino.

Which, though?

Think, think. If I study the junk in the car, surely that will supply clues. Even Kate, scrupulous housewife, keeps her car a slum. In the central cubby-hole are:

one glove
pair of sunglasses, broken
half tube of Polo mints, stuck together
a strip of Green Shield stamps
tissues, variously stained
one ordinary stone
one Belgian franc
remains of a chocolate biscuit
what may once have been an Alka-Seltzer tablet
two apple cores

On the floor are more tissues and, ah, some cigarette ends and one squashed cigarette packet, Embassy Filter. That would rule out Kate except that she takes her friends shopping, including Sue Kennerly who smokes like a chimney, likewise Max. In the back I can just see crumpled children's comics and a grubby tee-shirt. That would have ruled out Veronica earlier if I'd thought, unless Tom has kids. The little radio doesn't seem to work but judging by the one I put in for Kate they never do, really. Wait a minute – in one of the Fiats I have driven lately it was hanging forlornly from its wires. That would have been Veronica's, though. If it had been Kate's I would have been irritated.

Licence disc? Expired last day of February. I remember renewing Kate's about then but she could have omitted to put the new one up yet. 'Haven't I?' she'd say. 'It's in my handbag then. I can never work those little plastic things. How are they supposed to stay on?' Equally it could be Binnie simply forgetful or too hard up. Didn't she say something about an M.o.T. test?

You would think there'd be some occupational evidence: samples of these awful cosmetics, perhaps; or if she still works at Broadbents, some Windsor parking tickets. Unless Broadbents have their own car park. Handling characteristics? Certainly the steering is less precise than with other of the innumerable Fiats I have driven lately, and now I think about it has been getting worse.

God, I'm so tired, can hardly keep my eyes open.

Fellow pulls up at the filling station in a Fiat 500. 'A gallon of petrol and quarter of a pint of oil,' he says. 'And shall I sneeze in the tyres for you?' says the attendant.

Mummy's car's got no petrol. Well, pop it in the boot of mine and we'll drop her off at the garage.

The rotten steering is getting wobblier and wobblier.

These two ladies in a Fiat 500 which broke down. One looked under the bonnet and said, 'No wonder, the engine's fallen out.' The other was peering in the back. 'It's all right, I've found the spare.'

There is also a nasty pull to the right.

Tanker overtakes with loud blastings of the horn. We are wandering about all over the shop.

It can only be a flat tyre. Will have to pull up on the hard shoulder.

That's the clincher: the spare is also flat and still coated with dried yellow mud.

From the picnic that day, you see.
Dear Binnie!

Later

What happened then was that while I was still trying to decide whether the nearer emergency phone lay ahead or behind, up scorched a police Jag, lights flashing and whirling, the SUSPICIOUS sign glowing redly. I suppose I did look bleary if not as bleary as now. Could they see my driving licence? Actually, no, I didn't have it with me. Any other means of identification? Which is when I discovered I'd left my wallet somewhere, presumably the boat, just possibly Le Provençal.

While one officer stonily conducted the interview the other was mooching round in that massively disinterested way of theirs. Inevitably he observed that the Road Fund Licence was out of date.

You try explaining to the law, especially at 7 a.m., that you're attempting to return what you thought was your wife's car but in fact is your friend's – that is, *her* friend's – which you have taken in error in order to retrieve one belonging to, um, this author of one's in London.

In the end they unbent and produced a foot pump and even insisted on wielding it themselves on the understanding I would only try to make the next exit and the nearest garage. In fact I plugged on all the way to Dino's yard. He wasn't there of course but I was fast becoming expert in helping myself. The only snag was that there was no sign of the third, or Veronican, 500. I stormed around and shook the door of his corrugated tin hut in blind rage. To my surprise it sagged open. I poked around guiltily for a couple of minutes, without any clear idea of what I was seeking before the obvious next step struck me. Dino's phone, I should have remembered earlier, was an extension from

167

his home, wherever that was. I kept my finger on the buzzer until I heard him answer.

'What do you want? Ow you there? Who is?'

'It's Godley, Signor Godley – you know, who brings Signora Godley's little car, and Signora Davies' car and yesterday—'

'Ah, *si*, *si*, Mister Golly. What you do in my shop?'

'The little Fiat *quincente* yesterday, with the blown gasket – gasketo—'

'*Si*, *si*. I feex.'

'But where is it?'

'I leave out last night, like she say.'

'Who say – I mean, says?'

'Meestress Davies, of course.'

'No, not that one. I've got that one. The other one.'

'Meestress Golly's? You take eet yourself—'

'No, not that one either, that's in London now and I've got to get it back. The one I brought in and *exchanged* for Signora Golly's – Godley's – with the finito gasketo.'

'No, that is Meestress Davies—'

'That's just what it *isn't*. Signora Davies was the flatto spare tyre which you kindly did not feex, or fix, because I've just—'

'She say spare 'as puncture but when I look is okay.'

'Dino, you've mixed them all up. All the Fiats – *misto*, *misto*.'

'So 'ow many frocking Fiats you bring me? Too many frocking Fiats for one man, eh?'

Etcetera, etcetera.

I'm guessing some of it, because Dino is hard enough to understand at the best of times, and his wife was shouting away in the background, and outside his den the cocks and hens were squawking to be let out of the old Buick. I propped the door back as best I could and drove round to the Beechway. The tyre was down again, in fact it was

168

pretty well down to the rim. The wheel shuddered and clanged and people on bicycles pointed, but outside the Davieses – thank God – stood a little blue Fiat, and what was nearly as helpful, no white Triumph.

Binnie came to the door in a fluffy dressing gown and slippers, piece of toast in hand. After an initial blink of surprise she couldn't have been more sporting, and laughed merrily as I tried to explain.

'I never noticed,' she said.

'Not even the keys?' I showed her Veronica's.

'Not even in the dark. Good God, *what* are they up to?'

Geoffrey had been away overnight, in Northampton. The kids and mummy were still in bed. The only thing was – how was she to get to Broadbents?

I'd already worked that out. 'It's perfectly simple. I'll give you Veronica's spare, and Veronica Kate's, then get a new tyre on your wheel for Kate.'

She looked a bit lost, so in a lather of activity I jacked up her Fiat and made the switch, all in ten minutes. Of course, I was more than somewhat grubby by the time I'd finished, so Binnie, bless her, sent me up to the bathroom to clean up while she brushed and pressed my trousers, though she might have warned me her mother was staying again, in which case I would obviously have closed the door. Then just as I was enjoying a welcome cup of coffee that Mollie Fox-Rogers had to come breezing in. Well, let them think what they will! The only thing that matters is that the Chiswick Flyover looms ahead on what must be the last – no, last but one – leg of this nightmare shuttle. In half an hour at the outside I shall be back at Lots Road. Veronica will have *her* car again, and this one indubitably is hers. See: the radio dangles from its wires; the two lovers swing incontinently from the ignition; the licence expired three months ago: in the cubby hole are many Metropolitan and City of London parking tickets, not to mention various

169

pills, tissues, red drawing chalk, a banana and a block of fivepenny postage stamps which seem to have been soaked in tea. There is also an egg on the back seat, but that may have been left there by one of Dino's hens.

Unless the lady has vanished again, which God forbid, I shall recover my wallet, I shall recover my wife's motor-car. At last I begin to see a gleam of light at the end of the tunnel.

April 2 (p.m.)

Spoke too soon. She was still there, Veronica, that is; also my wallet; also Tom. There was coffee, lukewarm instant. There was champagne, lukewarm. I was greeted as the heavensent part-answer to an irritating problem, namely to find two witnesses for the marriage ceremony at Chelsea register office which Tom had arranged for ten a.m., preparatory to their flying off to Cork. During the coming and going which Veronica had suspected he had applied for the licence, which process apparently doesn't need both parties, and now had simply turned up with it. It is the spontaneous action fashionable with the young today. What would have happened if he had made it an hour earlier, or I had left an hour later, is a moot point.

As it was, I was too queasy from instant coffee and warm champagne and no food for fourteen hours to speculate on what might have been. When the happy couple drove off to their airport I was chiefly agitated to ensure they took the right car. Terence, the old queer off *Esmeralda IV*, was the other witness. The bride wore a light green two-piece suit with matching accessories.

At the office the big news was that another writ had arrived, from a real Mr Bodger the builder, in Bridgwater, Somerset, and who likewise claims he is being held up to ridicule, scorn and contempt. Even more ominously, if possible, there were urgent messages to ring Kate at home.

She said, 'What did you do with Rastus?'

'What do you mean?' – trying to remember.

'I've just fetched him from the police station covered in mud.'

'I think I put him out and forgot to call him in—'

'They also seemed to be expecting you to call in with your driving licence.'

'Well, you see—'

'And where's Janet's bike?'

'Oh, that's at Dino's.'

'Dino or whatever you call him has been telephoning.'

'Oh yes?' – but with sinking heart.

'Something about my car and Binnie Davies's car and someone else's car, none of which I understood—'

'I was about to say—'

'Except that you've obviously been up to something.'

'Honestly—'

'And as a matter of interest, where *is* my car?'

'I'm bringing it back this evening.'

'I think you better had. Together with a few explanations. You weren't home last night and you've not touched any of the food I left you.' And with a sort of sob she rang off.

Mrs Cernik was beside herself with satisfaction. 'Chust to hear Mr Godley trying to talk himself out of these dreadful things,' she will be relaying even now to the daughter. 'I tell you it made vun vince. Every word poor Mrs Godley is saying is as clear as I am saying to you.'

Is this the sixth or eighth or tenth flog along the linear limbo of the motorway? I've long lost count.

The airport and the airport hotels grind by. One is round, one is long and low, one is huge and red and blind.

Perhaps I should end it all: it would need only a flick of the wheel to drive headlong into a bridge pier or something.

171

In a Fiat 500 against the wind? Prickwell man's M-way suicide bid: nose feared broken.

At least it's finally the right Fiat. The moulting spider hangs from the key. The licence is actually valid. In the cubbyhole are felt-tip pens, a tiny broken torch, a lacy handkerchief, a strip of Disprins, a hymn book and a toothbrush. Among the books littered in the back I recognize *Ant and Bee* and *On the Farm* and – already – *Stanley the Suburban Squirrel*.

It is your car, all right.

It is you I'm talking to, at last.

Chapter Fourteen

April 4

I keep trying to tell you, you've got it all wrong. If only you would stop leaping to conclusions. There was this absurd muddle with the Fiats, which one day I'll elaborate into a saga to keep a dinner party in fits of laughter but which reduces in essence to the fact that I had to zoom back to London in a hurry and thought I'd collect your car from Dino's. In the rush I accidentally took the wrong one.

All right, it happened to be Binnie's. It could just as easily have been anyone's.

Forget about the gasket or whatever Dino was waffling about. There is nothing wrong with your gaskets. As for the tyre, I've already said I'll buy you a new one.

I had been looking forward to the shepherd's pie you left, honestly. Was just about to pop it in the oven. One would hardly choose a quick hamburger in a run-down café in Fulham instead, would one? I had to go because Tom and Veronica had their mad idea to get married and fly off to Ireland in the morning and it was necessary to see her first about these wretched libel actions. Incidentally there is now a third threatening letter in, from a Mr Bodgem – with an 'm' – who's a builder in Liverpool 18.

I can't understand why you find this part so difficult to believe. I did go all the way to London. I did not know, then, that I was going to be asked to be a witness next day. That was very much an off-the-cuff invitation. A wedding feast would not, in any case, have been a very suitable occasion on which to discuss lawsuits.

At least you can't doubt I had a puncture, having made a great fuss over the tangible evidence of it. That the spare should also have been flat, I thought we agreed, was entirely typical of the owner.

Late at night, it was no good thinking of help, especially as you had taken the A.A. card. Tom and Veronica very sportingly let me doss down in that studio place at the front – or in the bow, I should say. I was up at first light and with the aid of a friendly policeman and a foot pump managed to hobble back with a couple of stops for more air on the way.

I put the spare on from your car because presumably Binnie would be needing hers to go to work. I took it round to the Beechway for the same reason – after all, I had taken the damned thing in the first place. I was dirty and dishevelled from changing wheels, etcetera. She very kindly offered to brush and press my suit while I had a wash. One was wearing Geoffrey's dressing gown simply to have a cup of coffee while she finished. That he had happened to have been away for the night has nothing to do with it. That she was also in a dressing gown is equally irrelevant. Don't you often have breakfast in yours?

Besides, the children and also Binnie's mother were in the house. Indeed Mrs Lines came down only a minute or two after I drew a chair up to the table, and just before Mollie Fox-Rogers breezed in. Why you should take so much notice of that trouble-maker I don't know. You were always running her down when we lived in Pipkin Lane. What a coincidence that she should have decided yesterday she just had to see you about the Preservation Society! And should laughingly mention her morning encounter.

On reflection I certainly don't believe that story about popping along to Binnie's to ask her to change a pair of slippers at Cayley's. She saw me outside and was plain nosey and, like everyone else in the Beechway, much too keen to judge others by her own behaviour. As for Mrs Lines making that remark about sometimes not being sure which is her son-in-law, me or Geoffrey – that was merely her stupid idea of a joke. She's like that.

You must believe me, please . . .

It is ludicrous to be in the doghouse for the one thing that DIDN'T happen. What's more, it's so *unfair*.

'You're . . . *pathetic*. That's it: pathetic and sneaky and hopeless. Second-rate! You can't even bring any style to your squalid little goings-on.'
And: 'Do you think I'm blind? Do you think I didn't have a pretty shrewd idea of what was going on? Do you think the whole of the Beechway, if not the whole of Prickwell, didn't? You couldn't even bother to be efficient about it!
And: 'I don't suppose it ever occurred to you that it won't be very pleasant for me to have that crowd laughing behind their backs at me—'
'Your back, it would be, actually.'
'What?'
'People laugh behind other people's backs, not their own—'
'Don't interrupt. And the children – hardly very pleasant for them, having all their schoolfriends whispering and giggling. You monster!'
'Honestly, I don't think you need worry about that—'
'*Shut up!*'
Your scorn rings in my ears still. How many hours of it were there last night? Three? Four? Then an hour of tears. I

175

slept, exhausted, in the spare room. Today, so far, it has been silence, silence like stone. I have heard your voice only when you made a telephone call, to whom I don't know. I have driven into Prickwell. In the absence of instructions to the contrary I have bought the customary Saturday sausages from the butchers, though only a pound as the children are away. I have collected your spare wheel and new tyre from Dino and put up with complex protestations from him and paid a bill of thirty-eight pounds in respect of every known Fiat 500 in the Home Counties.

If I told you all, about Veronica and the truth about Binnie as well, would that resolve it once and for all, like the nitro-glycerine bravely flung into the oil-well fire – an explosion to blow out a conflagration? I'm tempted, I'm tempted.

Later

But when I got back a dark green car stood outside the Kennerlys', with army markings and a little red plate down by the bumper bearing a metal star. A soldier in uniform came out of the house carrying a valise and other odds and ends which he stowed in the boot.

I said, 'Max must be next door,' but you made no answer.

Only when he poked his head in to say goodbye did you speak again. For a few minutes everything was just as it had been, at least on the surface. We all smiled, chatted, glanced at the clocks and watches. Max and the driver and I shared a Quart of Tolly, you declined a sherry. We even had a rueful laugh over the *Stanley* libels. Max said breezily, 'They'll come to nothing, I'm sure.'

Of course I didn't know then what I know now.

I thought he looked very fit and though in civilian clothes – we have never seen him in uniform, do you realize? – somehow more soldierly. It's strange that Sue should not have wanted to be there to help him pack and so on, but after twenty-five years of comings and goings perhaps one treats them more casually. I wondered if I ought to take your hand or put my arm round you as we waved him off, but decided not to risk a rebuff. Did you notice how the driver, who had been quite at ease and chatty in our kitchen, instinctively became an 'other rank' again as he stood almost to attention to open the car door for Max. We went back in.

I said 'Shall I put the sausages on?'

'If you like.' At least you were still speaking. But you went upstairs and when you came down again you had changed into your nice trouser and reefer jacket outfit and carried the little tartan suitcase I bought you to take to Amsterdam in 1968.

Without preamble you said, 'I'm going back to mother and father's now. I'll bring the children back on Friday, by which time' – you swallowed – 'by which time I hope to have a better idea of what to do.'

'About what?'

'About us. Meanwhile you can do what you like and with who you like. Move her in here, if you want – as long as both of you are gone by the time we get back.'

'Aren't you staying for the sausages?' seemed to be the first thing I needed to know.

'I couldn't eat anything' – though in fact you were already cutting yourself a sandwich.

Nothing more was said until you had made the sandwich and poured yourself a glass of milk. It has always been the same when I'm in disfavour, you want to go teetotal. 'There is something else I am going to tell you,' you began at last.

If I try to remember exactly how you put it, I won't catch the directness, the flatness, the economy. But if I turn it into reported speech – I've just tried under my breath – I can't stop it sounding whiny, as if I were quoting your own words against you in an argument.

You said, more or less, 'It's about Max. Did you know he was . . . that he is very fond of me?'

'Of course, just as we are—'

'No more than whatever you're going to say. More than just fond neighbours. In love with me, I mean.'

Shamefully, my first reaction was to wonder how I could turn the revelation to advantage. The second, which is the one that doesn't go away, was a sort of pang in the abdomen.

'He never said as much, of course. Not until a few days ago, at least. But a woman can tell. It was flattering and . . . rather nice, as long as it went no further, which it didn't because he was much too honourable and I was much too stupid.' You speculated for a while. 'The retirement business made us both think about it a bit more, then this posting to Belfast much more.' You paused again. 'On Thursday, when I went to see Sarah's baby I could have come home, quite easily. But Max was there, too. I offered him a lift. On the way he suggested stopping for dinner. That's when I rang you, just to get the technical problem out of the way, so I could be free to concentrate on the real decision we were going to have to make.

'We had a nice dinner. It was at Letchworth of all places; the Letchworth Hall Hotel. Max was in fine form. We laughed a lot. Then he grew quieter and he started to tell me what I already knew and propose what I was already expecting. We discussed it very honestly. And very sensibly. And sensibly I decided that it would be . . . kind of belittling for us, and him especially, and Sue and you and everyone. So he said he'd catch a train to London and I said no, he wouldn't, and we drove there and I dropped him off at his club and came on out here, which was then about midnight, to an empty house, not even the bloody dog.'

You sat in silence for another minute, perhaps. Then picked up the tartan case and went out. I ran after you to tell you to take the big car again, but you were already fastening the safety belt in the little Fiat.

No good brooding, got to work. That's the thing, work. There's *Action Padre* I never did anything about. I'll do him this weekend, do him now. Get out set of drawings to present to Walter and then to the manufacturers. Janet's got paper and ink and felt-tips, nice bright and bold colours. I can do all the different uniforms and gear, not forgetting the vestments he carries to pop on for quick last rites or battlefield communion. Would he have different colours for the different seasons of the calendar, like old Lumsden and this new chap?

If I say he does, he does. And a Jeep or scout car with a little purple plate down by the bumper on it, a cross. That would be good.

Chapter Fifteen

April 5

The house is silent. I slept disgracefully well and when I awoke the ache had gone. Of course, it came flooding back as I remembered everything, which is always the worst part, the opposite of when you wake up with the despair and gradually it sinks in that it was all a dream and one didn't really get caught stealing nighties in Marks and Spencer.

Downstairs the drawing-room was littered with the *Action Padre* drawings – well, where else would one draw but a drawing-room? They were pitiful. Jane's felt-tips had mostly run out. Miranda must have taken hers with her, Little Sam's were dry because he had left the caps off, or had squashed and flattened tips. What colours I had been able to find were all wrong. I threw the lot in the waste bin. There was also an empty litre of Charbonnier Rouge which I seemed to have consumed along with the remains of the shepherd's pie and the sausages.

Today is the end of the financial year. Tomorrow Mrs Cernik and I are due to start assembling the documents for the accountant. That it is also the end of the faithless year goes without saying. I am going to complete the last tape on this little gadget. It has only a few minutes to run. And when you come back you shall listen to the whole saga. It won't be very pleasant for either of us, but that way there will be no secrets left to me, no illusions left to you. And without illusions to maintain or secrets to protect there's no game.

Among your records I found a sleeve I hadn't seen before. The drawing is of a bearded man with little oval spectacles. The name is Erik Satie, which I have heard often enough on the radio without registering anything about him. His pieces are called by such queer names as *Trois Gymnopédies* or 'a piece in the shape of a pear'. Listen, the plonking music fills the house, not itself at all funny, in fact rather grave and full of resignation. If I shut my eyes it could be Max playing except that even I can tell this pianist has a calm, a certainty, that eluded Max.

When I picture you together in that hotel dining room I get a little hollow spasm deep down inside. Yet I can't help feeling much closer to Max now. It is consoling to know that he is . . . well, like the rest of us. He was just too good to be true, and impossible to live next door to – a kind of standing paragon of kindness, humour, patience, understanding and all the other things I lacked. He never lost his temper or came home late or raged about the traffic out of London. He took Sue out to dinner every week and took his boys sailing. He was marvellous with Sarah when she was so difficult. I see him still in the garden after the wedding, saluting the General, kissing Kate, making that wry Brahmin gesture to the abominable Best Man.

Also, it is rather flattering that he should have fallen for my choice of wife. If you had decided otherwise that night, perhaps I would be insanely jealous. But just now the little hollow spasm seems to be of sympathy more than anything else. I know the . . . giantness, to you, of the decision you had to take and which I hardly thought about.

I wish sometimes you could take things more lightly. If anything happened to Max in Ulster, and of course that'd be unlikely, because he's much too senior to be in the firing line, but if it did – I would feel he had been cheated of something, and it was my fault.

In our bedroom the music still sounds clear and plaintive, though far off. The sun streams in through the window that looks over the heath. Spring is really here at last.

On the dressing table are your comb, brush, looking glass – no, let us be more specific: Victorian circular shaving companion, approx. twenty-two inches diameter, two hinged lids, pedestal appears to have been cut down. Silver-backed hairbrush, Walker and Hall, *circa* 1930, formerly the property of the vendor's Aunty Rose. Small swing-mirror in fruitwood . . . yes, it's the game we used to play at bedtime when we were first furnishing Pipkin Lane and haunting the auction sales.

Also: the Milk of White Rose and Almonds hand cream I have to fetch you from Jacksons in Piccadilly, the Calèche spray, the Crêpe de Chine toilet water, the phial of perfume which alone among the scents you use is not fresh and flower-like but has a musky, secret fragrance.

A necklace of pale, bony beads is where you put it down, together with the ivory or bone brooch you sometimes match against this: on the long seat, folded but – exceptionally for you – not put away, the soft blue pullover you were wearing until you changed to go. The wool still holds something of you.

On the chest of drawers are propped photographs of Janet, of Miranda, of Sam, of me, of us all together and in ones and twos, but mostly of the children and school photographs at that, so they have comic expressions and the colours are bright and hard and there is the same teddy bear or toy gramophone or vase of flowers in each. On the bedside table is your little stack of poetry books and a library book and a Penguin *Far From The Madding Crowd* and an envelope on which you have made a shopping list and a belt buckle and a teaspoon and a wrapped cough sweet. I am surrounded by the evidences of you.

There was never any real danger, if you did but know. We're in it too deeply together, we share too much in common: five thousand nights in the king-size bed that was our first extravagance – think of it this way, said the salesman, you spend a third of your lives there, don't you? Five thousand driftings off to sleep, a few times when one or both didn't, from tension or grievance or sickness; and all the wakings up to summer light or cold winter alarm clock or my feeling amorous or your feeling like a cup of tea.

When you think about it, there is something fantastically selfless about a girl getting married. She entrusts her whole life, all she might be, to this unknown chancer who is supposed to provide for her.

As Veronica put it, we are too married. It is weird that you still don't suspect what was going on there – or perhaps prefer not to suspect same, knowing it to be a far greater threat. Well, it *was* flattering, and exciting. Just to toy with the idea of abandoning the kind of life I had always led for one so foreign and unpredictable was like being offered a journey to the Moon. But she wanted love and I'm not much good at love; got rather good at the other thing, no better at love.

Not that the other thing is as indispensable as they make out. What is it but that definition Miranda found, giggling, in her school dictionary for another function altogether? – a small explosion between the legs. That's it: a small explosion more or less between the legs.

The real attraction, especially with Binnie, was that it was all nicely furtive. As with the secret bakehouse buns and coffee when I was a recruit, it was the stolen-ness of the stolen pleasures that mattered most, not the pleasures themselves. There is a case for quick half-hours in curtained rooms. To be open and honest and naked and unashamed is fine only as long as the sun doesn't show up the stretch marks, or the wind and the rain bring out the goose pimples. Poor Binnie, it was never the same after that. But at least she was cheerful, she didn't take pills, she liked a drink, she didn't have inky-bitten fingers, she didn't expect love.

The telephone was Walter, alive with good tidings. His Q.C. friend had assured him that the existence of three libel suits from three different plaintiffs each claiming to be identified with the same fictitious character is the perfect defence to any one of them. We need only to pit lawyer against lawyer and all will be settled modestly out of court.

This is cheering news, one must say. One can build again on such foundations. We must press on with the Ulster game, we must finish the *Stanley* sequel. If Veronica is too busy, never mind. As it was she who landed us in trouble it would in any case be better to go it alone. After all, it was our idea in the first place.

What a lovely morning! It is good to be alive. One might take Rastus for a run on the heath, and perhaps drop by at the Browsden Arms for a noggin and a chat with any of the old gang who happen to be there. On second thoughts, incidentally, I think it would be unkind and unnecessary to inflict these meanderings on you. The last tape has only a few inches left. One might deposit the whole lot out of harm's way somewhere; it would be something to play over to oneself when one is seventy!

Rastus – walkies!

Stanley went bobbity-bobbity along the topmost branch of the big walnut tree.

He looked down through the leaves with his big bright eyes.

'I'll have the skin off you yet,' shouted red-faced Mr Bodger the Builder.

'Supper is ready,' called Shirley Squirrel as she stirred the acorn soup.

But Stanley saw the flash of Selena's little bushy tail as she disappeared pippity-pippity into her nest in the chestnut-tree.

Stanley leaped WHE-EEEEEE through the air to land on the swaying tip of its outstretched-most branch. Bobbity bobbity bobbity he scampered towards the trunk. Tiddle-tiddle-tiddle, he slithered down it, stopping only to pick the two sweetest, juiciest hazel nuts from his secret hidey store.

'Nuts,' he sang to Selena.

'Nuts!' he said to the acorn soup.

'NUTS!!' he cried to Mr Bodger the Builder, and to the world.

Postscript

There the recordings ended. The last cassette had been wrapped in a page-proof from the children's book. Plucky old Stan, never down for long. Poor old Stan, he never took Shirley Squirrel sufficiently into account. Friends from Prickwell days kept us posted, of course, if they called by or had occasion to ring up. The Godleys had gone their separate ways, though no one was quite sure where these led. It would have made a neater dénouement, I suppose, if we had heard nothing at all until a chance encounter last year. We stopped for lunch at a small hotel in the Shires, and I think both of us recognized about the same time the graceful woman who directed us to the dining-room. 'It's Kate Thingummy,' my wife hissed. She must have remembered us, too, because when she bustled into the room with another party she looked our way and gave a little, guarded smile.

She came over and sat down while we were having coffee. After inquiring about the meal (which was very good) she said, 'You know that Graham and I broke up?' We made the usual noises. She was subdued, not very forthcoming. The hotel came to her when her mother died, and that was what had decided her, finally, to make the break. She had the children in term-time. Graham was supposed to have them in the holidays, but had been in Australia for six months. Ironically, he was working for Zillah Graves now. She straightened the already-perfect place setting in front of her and said, 'It wasn't getting any better, you see.'

'He had changed, though, hadn't he?'

She looked at me carefully. 'Yes he had. That was the trouble.'

'How do you mean?'

'He started being all forthright and honest. It didn't leave much to go on. I mean that – well, we all need our little pretences, don't we? Mine was that Graham was too stuffy to go off the rails. Suddenly I couldn't be sure any more. Besides, it made me very fond of him, the way he was.' She blinked, rather close to the tears that are always more touching in a self-possessed person.

'Did you know that he had been keeping a sort of diary, on tape?'

'Afterwards, yes.'

'Have you ever heard it?'

She shook her head. 'No point.'

'Would you be interested in reading a transcript?'

'If you like.'

She sent it back after a fortnight, with a note:
Thanks for letting me see the enclosed. I must say you've covered everyone's tracks jolly well. If you want to publish it, why not? That might be what he has been wanting all along. It might round off whatever he was trying to sort out. I don't know. If your hear from him at all, tell him Shirley Squirrel is still stirring the acorn soup, and it's supper time any time he cares to drop by.

Over to you, Stan. And for your share of the royalties, if any, contact me, care of the Society of Authors.